Raves for Julie Kenner and her novels!

"Great fun; wonderfully clever." —Jayne Ann Krentz,
New York Times bestselling author of *Running Hot*

"What would happen if Buffy the Vampire Slayer got married, moved to the suburbs, and became a stay-at-home mom? [A] sprightly, fast-paced ode to kick-ass housewives . . . Readers will find spunky Kate hard not to root for in spheres both domestic and demonic."
—*Publishers Weekly*

"A fabulously fun heroine . . . [an] ingenious literary creation." —*Booklist*

"It's a hoot." —Charlaine Harris, *New York Times* bestselling author of *From Dead to Worse*

"Smart, fast paced, unique . . . a blend of sophistication and wit that has you laughing out loud."
—Christine Feehan, #1 *New York Times* bestselling author of *Murder Game*

"Tongue-in-cheek . . . fast pacing and in-your-face action. Give it a try. Kate's a fun character and keeps you on the edge of your seat." —SFReader.com

"Kenner is at her irreverent best . . . delightfully amusing."
—*The Best Reviews*

"You're gonna love this book! Lots of humor and crazy situations and action." —*Fresh Fiction*

THE
GOOD GHOULS' GUIDE
TO GETTING EVEN

JULIE KENNER

ACE BOOKS, NEW YORK

THE BERKLEY PUBLISHING GROUP
Published by the Penguin Group
Penguin Group (USA) Inc.
375 Hudson Street, New York, New York 10014, USA

Penguin Group (Canada), 90 Eglinton Avenue East, Suite 700, Toronto, Ontario M4P 2Y3, Canada
(a division of Pearson Penguin Canada Inc.)
Penguin Books Ltd., 80 Strand, London WC2R 0RL, England
Penguin Group Ireland, 25 St. Stephen's Green, Dublin 2, Ireland (a division of Penguin Books Ltd.)
Penguin Group (Australia), 250 Camberwell Road, Camberwell, Victoria 3124, Australia
(a division of Pearson Australia Group Pty. Ltd.)
Penguin Books India Pvt. Ltd., 11 Community Centre, Panchsheel Park, New Delhi—110 017, India
Penguin Group (NZ), 67 Apollo Drive, Rosedale, North Shore 0632, New Zealand
(a division of Pearson New Zealand Ltd.)
Penguin Books (South Africa) (Pty.) Ltd., 24 Sturdee Avenue, Rosebank, Johannesburg 2196,
South Africa

Penguin Books Ltd., Registered Offices: 80 Strand, London WC2R 0RL, England

This is a work of fiction. Names, characters, places, and incidents either are the product of the author's imagination or are used fictitiously, and any resemblance to actual persons, living or dead, business establishments, events, or locales is entirely coincidental. The publisher does not have any control over and does not assume any responsibility for author or third-party websites or their content.

THE GOOD GHOULS' GUIDE TO GETTING EVEN

An Ace Book / published by arrangement with the author

PRINTING HISTORY
Berkley Jam trade paperback edition / April 2007
Ace mass-market edition / April 2009

Copyright © 2007 by Julie Kenner.
Cover art by Chad Michael Ward.
Cover design by Lesley Worrell.
Interior text design by Kristin del Rosario.

ISBN: 978-0-441-01704-1

ACE
Ace Books are published by The Berkley Publishing Group,
a division of Penguin Group (USA) Inc.,
375 Hudson Street, New York, New York 10014.
ACE and the "A" design are trademarks of Penguin Group (USA) Inc.

PRINTED IN THE UNITED STATES OF AMERICA

10 9 8 7 6 5 4 3

To Zoe.
Thanks for doing my "market research."

PROLOGUE

If he weren't already dead, I swear I would kill Stephen Wills. I mean, the undead jerkwad completely ruined my sixteenth birthday. It's one thing not to get the car my dad promised me, but to be turned into a *vampire*? I'm sorry, but that's taking bad karma to a whole new level.

But maybe I'm getting ahead of myself. My name is Elizabeth Frasier and I'm sixteen years old (dead?). I'm a junior at Waterloo High in Austin, Texas. Or, at least, I was a junior until I woke up dead in a field behind the school. I'm pretty sure that the Austin Independent School District's budget doesn't cover the education of the undead.

Austin, you might be interested to know, has the largest urban colony of Mexican free-tailed bats in the world. I've known that fact for years. More recently, I've learned that Austin has a pretty hefty population of teenage vampires. Coincidence? I think not.

The thing is, I don't believe in coincidences. I believe in cause and effect, setup and payoff. I've spent almost sixteen years' worth of weekends parked in front of a movie screen, and I know that it's always the stupid coincidences that have the audience groaning and throwing popcorn. But make the stupid coincidence part of a bigger plan, and we're right there on the edge of our seats.

It's like that in life, too. Something might *look* like a coincidence, but it's probably part of some overall scheme. Just because you don't see the big picture doesn't mean it's not there. And if you don't watch out, you might end up getting burned.

So you see, I should have realized. I should have *known*. But this is Stephen Wills we're talking about. Hunky, gorgeous, dreamy Stephen Wills. And all I can do is plead temporary insanity.

It started, like so many things in high school, during lunch . . .

CHAPTER 1

"Are you going to eat your banana?" Jenny was staring mournfully into the purple Container Store lunch sack that her mom had packed for her that morning.

We were in our usual seats at a small table tucked in the corner of the cafeteria, near the window that overlooked the faculty parking lot. The table sat six. Two chairs had been dragged away for a cluster of boys who had their Game Boys wired together and were getting down and dirty with some game or other.

The other two chairs were empty. I expected they'd stay that way. It's not that Jenny and I weren't popular. (Well, we weren't, but that's not the point.) It's just that we were average. And we'd been snagging this table for ourselves for the last two years. I edit the school newspaper, and Jenny's our weekly columnist, so we usually had articles and pictures spread all over the place.

Jenny also writes the *Waterloo Watch*, an anonymous blog that's hugely popular. But I'm the only one who knows about that. And since Jenny can't reveal herself as the brains behind the *Watch*, she's gotten no coolness mileage out of the blog at all.

Which is too bad, really. Because at the moment, the whole school's all hyped up with this Voice of Waterloo contest to pick a guy or a girl who'll be the on-campus reporter for a news segment one of the local television stations is starting.

The *Waterloo Watch* has been running a poll, but I hardly needed to see it to guess who was winning. Either Stephen Wills or Tamara McKnight. Why? Because only one month ago they were elected homecoming king and queen. And, honestly, the student body just isn't that imaginative.

Even so, Jenny swears that we have a shot, too. Her theory is that because we control who's in the news, that makes us cooler than the kids in the popular cliques.

"We have the power," she's always saying. "And that makes us *sooooo* much cooler than Stephen Wills and Tamara McKnight and their whole crowd."

Um, whatever.

It's sort of like the whole tree-falling-in-a-forest thing: if you're popular but nobody knows, are you really popular at all?

I'm thinking the answer is no.

I passed Jenny the banana, then shoved my uneaten tuna sandwich back into the sack and crumpled it up. I *so* wasn't up for food right now.

"So why aren't you eating lunch?" I asked, nodding toward her lunch sack. "Nothing good in there?"

"Peanut butter." She made a face. "My mother's sole purpose in life is to torture me. She knows this stuff is loaded with calories. I'll be the size of a blimp if I eat this."

Since Jenny was about as big around as Lindsay Lohan after a fit of bulimia, I wasn't terribly worried about her impending blimpiness.

"Trade?" she asked, starting to peel the banana.

I shook my head. "Can't eat. Nervous." I'd missed first and second periods in order to audition for one of the drill team's replacement slots, and I was counting down the minutes until the faculty advisor posted the names of all the girls who were getting a callback.

"I still can't believe you actually auditioned," Jenny said, since I'm not exactly the drill team type even though I've taken dance and gymnastics since I was three years old. "My mom wanted me to, and I told her I wouldn't even consider participating in such a sexist, antifeminist ritual." Jenny's all about sniffing out and eradicating sexism.

I shrugged. "Yeah, well, you know." Just so the record's straight, the drill team hasn't ever been a huge ambition of mine, but right now I'm all about rounding out my transcript. I've got the academic thing down with my grades and three years of AP science and math classes. And I've got the leadership thing down with the school paper. All of which sounds really good if you're chatting with your grandparents, but I knew my application needed more. I needed something on there that proved I didn't have to be the one in charge. Colleges like to see that you're a team player. That's very, very important. All the how-to books say so.

Even my mom (who's a pain about most things) is totally behind my crusade to up my college appeal. My mom's a trial attorney, and her motto is that you can never be too careful or too prepared. Which was why she made me take my SATs early, and then apply to a ton of in-state schools so I'd have something lined up if the Shangri-la of higher education turned me down.

Now I've got conditional acceptance letters and one early admission invitation from four schools in Texas. But those are only my backup plan. My Shangri-la is the Tisch School at NYU (with UCLA and USC running close behind). True, I hadn't informed my parents of the whole Tisch Is Nirvana plan, but that was just a minor oversight. Because no matter how much my parents might be gunning for me to be a doctor or a lawyer, I just didn't see that happening. Instead, I was going to make great movies. I saw myself as the next Steven Spielberg, but without the scraggly beard and baseball cap. Or the next Coen Brothers, only without the sibling. Or Sofia Coppola. Only with, you know, a plot.

Whatever. The point is, I want to get accepted to Tisch, and that meant I was doing everything—*everything*—to make sure my application was so stellar that there was no way they could turn me down. (Technically, I think they can now turn me down for being dead. Which sucks. And which is why Stephen Wills was going to pay big-time. But while I was waiting for drill team callbacks that day, I was still blissfully alive and unaware of my impending vampiness.)

I needed a perfect college application, and that meant extracurriculars, and that meant drill team.

Which is why I was totally stressing about whether I'd made the team.

"I hate this," I told Jenny. And I did, too. I always know how I did on tests and stuff. But right then, I had no clue what was going to happen, and it was making my stomach jump around in a really unpleasant way.

"So, are you too nervous to eat anything at all?" Jenny

asked, and this time when I looked up she was holding a chocolate cupcake with a single candle. "Happy birthday!"

"Oh, man!" Honestly, I thought I was going to cry. "No one else remembered."

"No one?" Her tone was bland, but I knew she understood. My parents divorced six months ago. You'd think I would have suddenly been their priority, but it hadn't worked out that way. Instead, they just shifted me between Mom's house and Dad's apartment and tried to pretend like everything was normal. Let me clue you in here: everything was far from normal. *Very* far.

"Whatever," I said, running my finger over the icing and then sucking it off.

"Maybe they're waiting until tonight. Your dad said he was getting you a car, right?"

"Sort of. Maybe. I'm not sure." A few months ago, my dad got me a part-time job in the lab of a nearby hospital where he has privileges, and last weekend he came into the lab and dropped some pretty heavy hints. But this was my dad we're talking about—a man who can remember the diagnosis of a patient from fifteen years ago, but can't remember to buy milk—so I knew better than to get my hopes up.

"Hmm," Jenny said.

"Hmm," I agreed. Then I took another fingerful of chocolate.

Jenny looked around the lunchroom, as if expecting my dad to drive a Mini Cooper into the room at any second. *"Beth!"* she whispered, whipping back so fast her ponytail smacked her in the face. "Ladybell just got here!" Ladybell is the drill team coach and—yes—that's really her name.

My stomach quit doing flips and started doing jazz hands,

fluttering so much that I thought I'd barf up the tiny bit of frosting I'd just ingested. *This is it,* I thought. *Fail, and my application's screwed.*

Even worse, it would be the first time I'd failed at anything at school.

And honestly, I wasn't really sure I could deal with that.

CHAPTER 2

My stomach lurched again as I wondered for the eighty-gazillionth time if I'd gotten a callback. I *had* to have made it. I was Beth Frasier, current class valedictorian (and I intended to stay that way, despite the fact that Clayton Greene was one measly little grade point behind me). I was the newspaper editor. I could dissect frogs, conjugate Latin verbs, and recite from memory every one of the Best Picture Academy Award winners. I'd taken first place in the State Science Fair for two years running, and I repeatedly beat my brilliantly geeky father at chess. I did *not* fail. And I really, really, really didn't want to be proven wrong by a grown woman named Ladybell.

Honestly, why was I doing this to myself? The uniforms were goofy, and did I really want every guy in school staring at my rear?

Okay, let's not answer that one. Just so I can keep an ounce of dignity.

At any rate, as soon as Ladybell left, Jenny and I started

forcing our way across the caf, which sounds a lot easier than it is, considering the student-to-square-foot ratio. I stopped and looked around, searching for a linear path to the bulletin board. That's when I saw Clayton Greene. I stiffened, then immediately relaxed. So what if he was there? I mean, it wasn't as if we were *graded* on lunch. And he had to eat, too, right?

I told myself that the funny feeling in my stomach came from unexpectedly seeing my GPA nemesis. What else could it be? Then I tapped Jenny's back and told her to move on. She told me that she couldn't because someone had spilled a tray and was bent over trying to pick up bits and pieces of congealed green Jell-O salad. Gross.

Since we were stuck, I let my eyes turn back to Clayton. This time, I told myself I was simply reconnoitering. After all, we were fighting for the valedictorian slot, right? It was my academic responsibility to keep an eye on him.

He was sitting at a table with some other kids, but he didn't look like he was *with* the other kids, if you know what I mean. Instead, he was hunched down, a book open in front of him and his lunch all but ignored.

While I was scoping out Clayton (all for the purpose of protecting my class rank), Chris Freytag and Ennis Walker approached his table. They're both on the football team, they both date cheerleaders, and they're both completely obnoxious. (And, yes, I realize that the idea of joining the drill team and doing dance routines to support these ob- noxious cretins is a bit hypocritical, but I had my transcript to think about.)

Actually, it's a miracle I recognized them at all. They both were wearing oversized burnt-orange sweatjackets em- blazoned with a picture of Bevo, the University of Texas's longhorn mascot. The jackets had hoods, and they had them up, covering their heads and hanging over to even cover their faces. Honestly, they looked like someone you'd see in a movie about South Central Los Angeles. Not in the cafeteria at Waterloo High.

I figured Ennis and Chris would pass right by Clayton's table (they're not exactly buds, if you know what I mean), but I was wrong. They stopped right across from Clayton, who didn't even look up. I smiled at that. Clayton might be my nemesis and a major geek, but he's as cool as they come.

Turns out, though, that they weren't interested in Clayton. Instead, Ennis accidentally-on-purpose dropped his Jell-O salad on Richie Carter's head. Richie's on the debate team and usually stars in the school musical. He's a nice guy, not one of "the" popular kids, but not shunned either.

He's also gay. Not that he advertises it, but everyone knows. Nobody cares. Well, except maybe for Chris and Ennis. But they're brain-dead jocks; the phrase "minding their own business" really wasn't all that familiar to them.

"Aw, man," I heard Ennis say, as green goo dripped down Richie's neck. "Sorry about that, dude."

"Come on, Ennis," Chris said. "He's not worth it."

"Not worth it? But look how funny he looks," Ennis said. "And isn't 'queer' another word for 'funny'?"

"Just like 'Ennis' is another word for 'asswipe,'" Richie said, sending a wave of shocked whispers coursing around the room.

"Whoa!" Jenny said.

"He's going to get his face smashed in," I said. Richie's a nice guy, but I was thinking common sense wasn't his strong suit. Not if he was provoking Chris and Ennis.

I started in that direction, then stopped as Clayton pushed his book aside. "Hey, Ennis," he said. "You've got some of that Jell-O on your jacket. Hang on, I'll get it for you."

And as a confused Ennis looked down at his pristine burnt-orange jacket, Clayton got up, walked around the table, grabbed an uneaten bowl of Jell-O off Richie's tray, and dumped it all over Ennis's front.

Ennis jumped back, hissing with rage. Honestly! The dude was *hissing*! And even with the shadows from the hood, I could see that his whole face shifted, like he was going to explode with anger. And I'm certain I'm not imagining it, because I saw Clayton jump, too. Then Clayton grabbed Richie's arm, pulled him up, and started to drag him out of the caf.

"You better haul ass, Clayton-queerboy," Ennis said. "This ain't over."

He jerked Chris's shoulders, and they both headed out the way they came, shoulders hunched, their backs and heads covered in burnt-orange sweatshirts.

"Whoa," Jenny said.

"Homophobic scum-sucking jerks," I muttered. "But man, I have to give Clayton his props. Did you see Ennis's face?"

"He was pissed."

"He was livid. But he also looked like he was on drugs or forgot to use his Proactiv or something."

Jenny cocked her head. "You know, I never see Ennis in first period anymore. Hungover? Strung out? Maybe the Waterloo Watcher should look into that. If he's using, it would be the Watcher's civic duty to report that to the masses."

She smiled, and I did, too. Because we both knew that even if Principal Phillips heard about the whole gay-baiting thing, Ennis would only get detention. But drug use? Well, that could cost Chris or Ennis their precious football.

We moved on then, toward the bulletin board, but I could tell Jenny's mind had drifted to her blog.

"What are they doing skipping classes and still playing football anyway?" I said, since my mind was still on the jerks.

Jenny rolled her eyes. "Coach Dunne probably hired tutors so his precious players could get their beauty sleep."

We both had a good laugh at that, because Chris and Ennis might be football gods, but they are *so* not beautiful.

After that laugh, though, I really did forget about Chris and Ennis. Because we'd reached the bulletin board. And all I could think about now was not throwing up.

CHAPTER 3

I tried to ignore the bodies jostling against me, as I let my eyes skim the list, searching for Frasier. Danziger, Dell, Evans, Falk, Fossen, Frost, Garrison—

What?

No, no, no. That could *not* be right.

"Well?" Jenny said, moving around behind me. "Are you there?"

I ignored her and started over, this time running my finger down the list, one name at a time. And I started with "A"—just in case the folks down there in the gym weren't real clear on how to alphabetize. No Frasiers. For that matter, no Beths or Elizabeths. Not from A to F. And not from F to Z.

The gymnasts in my stomach stopped flipping, morphing suddenly into solid, lead bricks. Bile rose in my throat, and I was certain I was going to be sick. Oh, God, I *really* was going to be sick!

I clapped my hand over my mouth and sprinted for the

door, shoving people aside and ignoring their protests. Jenny pounded after me, slamming into the girls' bathroom just as I shut myself up in the handicap stall.

"Beth? Beth! What happened?" Jenny was pounding on the door, but I wasn't answering because I was too busy holding my stomach and trying not to barf. "Holy crap, Beth! Are you okay?"

This time, Jenny's voice came from above me, and I looked up to see her peering over the side of the stall, obviously standing on the toilet next door.

I took a few deep breaths. "Yeah. I just—bad tuna fish, maybe."

"Mmmm."

I almost asked what she meant by *that*, but her head disappeared, and I remembered too late that I hadn't actually touched my sandwich. I opened the stall door, and there she was again. I pushed past her toward the sink and splashed water on my face, all the while telling myself I was being pathetic. Unfortunately, my earnest little talk with myself wasn't making me feel any better about being a total abject failure.

"It's Ladybell," Jenny said gently. "She probably hates you. I mean, she has to have read all those editorials you wrote last year."

I nodded in agreement, hardly able to believe I'd ruined my chances for college by calling the drill team a robotocized group of Stepford Teens. I mean, sure, *now* I saw the error of my ways. But back then I'd had no idea I might actually want to join the cult.

"She shouldn't have taken it personally," I said. "I was only trying to incite the masses."

"Authority figures hate it when you incite the masses," Jenny said knowingly. Honestly, I think she had a point.

I drew in a breath, then smoothed my Tisch sweatshirt and wondered if that was as close as I'd ever get.

"Nobody in New York cares about drill teams," Jenny said, trying to be kind. "And your transcript's so full up they probably wouldn't have even noticed one more extracurricular anyway."

I shrugged, but it was halfhearted. Jenny was trying to be nice, but I knew the truth: the Nirvana That Is Tisch notices everything. They have to. The school is highly competitive. And it's the little things that make the difference. If I didn't have drill team, I'd have to figure out something else. But what?

I had no idea, and right then I didn't have the energy to think about it. I'd think about it tomorrow after my ego had (hopefully) recovered a little.

"We've got class in fifteen," Jenny said. "Are you going to be okay?"

"Sure," I said, with more confidence than I felt.

I started for the door, but Jenny held me back, then proceeded to doctor my face with the contents of her makeup kit. She says she doesn't care about the fake ideal of beauty foisted upon us by Madison Avenue, but she still carries half of Sephora in her purse. She wiped off my smeared mascara, added some blush, and passed me a pot of lip gloss. I dabbed some on and reluctantly agreed that I didn't look quite as pale, forlorn, and despondent. That's the miracle of modern cosmetics—it totally erases all real emotion and makes women presentable to the world as happy little Stepford beings. (Okay, yes, I was still feeling surly about not getting called back.)

I reached out to grab the door, only to jump back as it was shoved forward, revealing Tamara McKnight in all her haughty, head-cheerleader glory. "Oh, hey," she said. "I thought I might find you in here."

That caught my attention. Because as far as I know, Tamara's never had a reason to look for me in her life. Well, except when she wants something published in the school paper.

"Um?" Okay, granted, that wasn't the most articulate of responses, but she caught me off guard. Plus, I wasn't exactly myself right then.

"Am I supposed to stand here all day?" Her cool blue eyes bored into me. *Man,* I thought, *does she really hate me that much?* But when I looked again I saw nothing but bland indifference. "Move over and let me in."

"Moving," I said. I stepped to the left, planning to go around her and out the door, but she put her arm out, blocking my path.

I gritted my teeth and told myself that she couldn't help being a bitch. She'd been overcome by the peroxide fumes from dyeing her hair since age five. "What do you want, Tamara?" I asked. "I'm really not in the mood."

"I guess not," she said, then stepped toward me. Since I'm all about personal space, I took a step backward. Behind her, the door swung closed, and there we were, Tamara, Jenny, and me, trapped in the girls' bathroom. How cozy.

Tamara glided to the mirror—honestly! The girl glides!— and started to check her perfect makeup on her perfect skin. I half considered making a dash for the door. But I was curious now and stayed put. "What do you want?" I asked again.

She squinted at the mirror, then worked the edge of her finger at a microscopic little smudge of mascara. "I hope you aren't too bummed. That you didn't get called back for the drill team, I mean."

"Right," I said. "Like you even care."

I heard Jenny make a little popping sound as she sucked in air. This was *not* the way I usually talked, even to people I consider the walking brain-dead. I'm *nice*. Everyone at Waterloo knows it. But today, I wasn't feeling it.

"God, Beth," Tamara said, actually deigning to turn away from her reflection and look at me directly. "What bug crawled up your butt?"

I was about to tell her that it was a bug named Tamara when the door opened again and Stacy Plunkett marched in, her raven hair pulled back in a clip. Stacy's all about her hair. Jenny managed to find out that Stacy's mom actually flies with her to some salon in Manhattan for haircuts. The story had been one of the most popular on the *Waterloo Watch* blog, and when someone asked Stacy about it in World Literature class, she just looked down her nose at them and said, "Well, of course it's true!"

Me, I usually end up at Supercuts.

"Come *on*, Tam," Stacy said. "What is taking so long?" Even though she was clearly irritated, she still managed to look bored. Actually, Stacy went through life looking bored. She's dating Chris now, but before they hooked up, I'd have to say that she'd had more dates in her almost-eighteen years than I expected to have in my entire life.

Still, in my moments of late-night angst, I sometimes practice Stacy's particular brand of ennui in the mirror. So far, I haven't quite gotten it right. I figure that's okay, because for all I know, the look causes some sort of brain degeneration. After all, Stacy's actually dating Chris Freytag. And if that's not evidence of diminished capacity, I don't know what is.

"I still can't believe we're doing this," Tamara said, more to herself than to me or Stacy. Why I was still standing there, I don't know. She wasn't talking to me anymore. But I'd been blessed with an audience with Queen Tamara, and once blessed, you don't walk away until dismissed. Or some such nonsense.

"Just get on with it," Stacy said. Her gaze shifted pointedly toward me. "Ask," she repeated.

That got me curious. "Ask what?"

"Just chill, Stace," Tamara said.

I held up a hand in a surrender gesture. Queen Tamara or not, this was getting old fast. "You guys have fun. I'm going to Latin." I turned and headed toward the door.

"I know why you didn't make the squad," Tamara said.

I stopped walking. "I'm listening," I said to the door.

That's when she dropped the bomb, igniting a flash of both fury and awe the likes of which I'd never really experienced before. "Because I told Ladybell not to let you on."

CHAPTER 4

"What?" In the space of two seconds I'd gone from violent anger to complete confusion. How could Tamara tell a teacher what to do? She had to be lying. I had no idea *why* she was lying, but I figured it probably had something to do with wanting her picture in the paper. Or maybe she wanted my help with chemistry. In the end, I was right—she *did* want something. But I'd been thinking way, way, way too small. She didn't want me to do something for her. She wanted *me*. Or, rather, Stephen Wills did.

Right then, though, I didn't know any of that, and so I just gaped and wondered and silently cursed, waiting for her to hurry up and explain what she was doing occupying space on my planet and breathing my air and generally making life miserable for nondivas everywhere.

"God, Beth," she said. "You don't have to look so pissed off. I was doing you a favor." She looked to Stacy, who started bobbing her head like some bobble-head toy.

"You know what? Don't do me any more favors."

She rolled her eyes. "Drill team's second string. You're looking to pump up your transcript, right? Sloppy seconds won't cut it." She leaned in toward the mirror again and ran a thumb under her eye, removing a microscopic dot of mascara.

"What's your point?"

"My point is that you're an idiot to want to be in the faceless pep parade when you could be on the front lines as a cheerleader."

Behind me, I could hear Jenny making choking sounds. "Excuse me?" I asked. This had to be some sort of cruel joke, but so far, I wasn't seeing the punch line.

"God, don't make me repeat it," Tamara said.

I held up a hand. "Wait. You dangle some cheerleading carrot in front of me, but now you don't want to talk to me about it?"

"She's still getting used to the idea," Stacy said, her Barbie-doll smile flashing a million watts my direction.

"Uh-huh," I said. "Not really feeling the love." I turned back toward the door just as the warning bell rang. One minute left to get to class. I grabbed the door handle.

"Wait," Tamara said, giving my arm enough of a jerk that she pulled me free of the door.

"Hey!"

"Look, we've never been the best of friends—"

"Best? We've never been friends at all!"

"But I'm serious," she continued, as if I hadn't said a word. "The squad could use you. We're competing this year, and you're good. Did you see *Bring It On*?"

I blinked, trying to follow the conversation. "Um, that cheerleading movie? Yeah."

"Well, you're like that girl. The one who played Faith on *Buffy*. You're kind of a misfit, but you're good. And we want to win. So we want you."

"Gee. With all the warm fuzzies, how could I say no?"

Stacy's lips were tight together and she was glaring daggers at Tamara. Beside me, Jenny was doing the exact same thing. Finally, Stacy spoke. "Look, Beth. We watched the drill team auditions because we need a replacement. Mary-Jo's dad transferred to California, and our alternate broke her leg. So we're serious when we say we want you. Aren't we, Tamara?"

Tamara nodded. She even conjured a smile. I felt the warm glow of acceptance. Not.

Before I could say anything, though, she nailed me with a stare. "So? Will you do it?"

"I don't know, I—"

"Of course she will," Jenny said, sidling even closer to me.

"What?" I made a motion between her and Tamara. "You were just—"

"I know, I know. But this is *cheerleading*. I mean, she may be the queen bitch from hell"—at that, she smiled sweetly at Tamara—"but, Beth, come *on*. Transcript. Rank. The whole shebang. I mean, duh."

Not the most articulate of persuasive speeches, but I got the message. Still, though, I wasn't convinced. I mean, it was one thing to be a relatively faceless member of the drill team. I could handle that level of school spirit.

Sort of.

Maybe.

So long as I kept the dream of Tisch close to my heart.

But to be one of six girls, right out front, cheering my little heart out? Honestly, I wasn't sure I could do that. Especially since I still haven't gotten through my head why I give a flip about an oblong ball being chased up and down a field by guys in tight pants who slap each other on the butt.

Plus, I had to consider the companion factor. I mean, I've listened to enough of their conversations (the Tamara types, I mean) to know that my mind would probably turn to mush and seep out my ears after only fifteen minutes. I mean, it's all "sale at Bebe" this and "new eyeliner from Sephora" that. I've never once heard them talk about anything substantive. Like, you know, whether George Lucas jumped the shark making episodes one through three. Or which is really the better show: *Buffy the Vampire Slayer* or *Firefly*. These are questions you can sink your teeth into. *Not* whether Nars or Cargo makes the better bronzer.

"Look," Tamara said, possibly realizing that I wasn't jumping at the opportunity to spend quality time with her every afternoon. "We really do want you." She sounded sincere, even if she looked like she was sucking on a lemon. "But you don't have to commit now. Why don't you come to practice after school? Stephen Wills and some other guys from the team are going to be there. You can check it out and then decide. And we'll probably go out for pizza or something afterward."

"Oh, man," Jenny said. "I am going to kill my mom for never making me take dance."

I understood the sentiment. Stephen Wills was a legend at Waterloo. Hollywood handsome, he was also a total football hero with a scholarship to somewhere that cared about that kind of thing. I didn't care. Like I said, I don't get football. But I will confess that he looks really nice in those ridiculous tight pants. And he's got the clearest blue eyes I've ever seen . . .

Honestly.

Here's how bad I had it for Stephen Wills: even though I would never—*ever*—admit it to Jenny, I actually voted for him for homecoming king. And even though I kind of secretly coveted the spot myself, since voting for me would be a waste of a vote, I planned to cast my ballot for Stephen Wills as the Voice of Waterloo, too.

So, yeah, Stephen's presence was a definite incentive.

Besides, I figured pizza with my man Stephen might be the one thing that could turn this crap birthday around. After all, everyone knew Tamara had the hots for him, but they weren't dating. Not officially, anyway. At least not officially enough to have made it onto the *Waterloo Watch* blog.

So maybe if he and I shared a little pizza . . .

I let my thoughts wander off, then stood there, feeling ridiculous. Lust, it seemed, really could make people stupid. Even me.

"Great," Stacy said, the second I breathed my agreement. "Meet us on the field after last period." And then she and Tamara disappeared out the door without a backward glance.

I didn't even have the mental energy to be irritated. I was too busy drooling on the floor and trying not to hit my head on the ceiling tiles as I floated on a little cloud of lust-filled happiness.

"Wow," Jenny said. Then kept repeating it over and over again. "Wow. Wow. Wow."

"Yeah," I said. "Wow." I looked at her sideways. "I thought you told your mom all this stuff was sexist and antifeminist."

She shrugged. "Well, yeah, sure. But that was drill team. Cheerleaders are popular. And it's Stephen Freakin' Wills we're talking about. I mean, the man is totally to die for."

And, as it turned out, that was very, very true.

CHAPTER 5

I coasted through my classes, then floated to my locker where Elise Lackland was waiting for me. Elise has had my sincerest admiration ever since she followed Chris Freytag into the boys' bathroom just so she could dump him.

Jenny blogged about it, and the story became the scandal of the moment at school the next day. (Everyone sided with Chris, of course. He's a Football God, and Elise is fifteen pounds overweight.)

"Hey," I said. "What's up?" I like Elise a lot. Whereas I consider Stacy an idiot for dating Chris, I think Elise is a freakin' genius for dumping him. According to Elise, Chris used to be a nice guy before he made the team. I'm a grade behind them, and so I have to take her word for it. Since I really do like her, I'm willing to give her the benefit of the doubt, even though I secretly think she's delusional.

She pulled her precalculus text out of her backpack and held it up to me. "I'm so lost. I know we're not scheduled to meet until next week, but please, please, please. If I fail, I'm going to be stuck taking summer school instead of going to London with my dad before college."

I almost laughed. I mean, I would have helped her even without the sob story. I do tutoring for extra credit (it's this whole complicated program the school set up a year or so ago), and the system is totally regimented. But like I said, I like Elise. If she was afraid of flunking, I'd totally help her out.

"Of course I'll help," I said. "But you were jamming the last time we got together. What happened?"

She shook her head. "I don't know. Everything's harder lately. I'd say it's spring fever, but since it's only November, I don't think that works. I just can't seem to stay awake." She yawned, as if to illustrate her point, then did an elaborate neck roll. I noticed a bandage there, almost below her ear and slightly back, now revealed by the swing of her hair.

"What did you do?" I asked, nodding at it.

"Who knows? Some bug. I drenched it in cortisone cream, so thank goodness it's not itching." She yawned again. "Maybe it's the time change. I don't know. All I know is I have to nail math. You'll help me, right?"

"I told you. Sure. When?"

"Now?"

"Um. Now is a little tricky." Considering the Stacy-Chris-Elise thing, I wasn't too keen on mentioning my upcoming cheerleader rendezvous. "How about lunch tomorrow?"

"Lunch," she repeated. "But you always eat with Jenny."

"Jenny can eat by herself," I said.

"I can?" Jenny asked, coming up beside us. I looked up and saw Tamara walking by. She lifted her eyebrows and tapped her watch. I nodded, just a little, but I saw Elise taking the whole thing in. I stifled the urge to tell Elise that she was seeing things and that I was *so* not talking with Tamara. But the thing is, I *was* about to become associated with the Queen Bitch and her hive. I might as well get used to the idea.

"Why am I eating alone?" Jenny asked, leaning past me into my locker to grab the bag of Doritos I'd shoved there.

"I'm tutoring Elise."

"Oh. Right. Whatever. So . . ." She cocked her head and I nodded.

"Listen, Elise—"

"You gotta go. Yeah. Sure." She made a little face, then glanced off in the direction that Tamara had gone. "So lunch tomorrow, right? You won't forget? The midterm's coming up, and—"

"I won't forget."

"Okay. Great. Thanks."

"It's so unfair," Jenny said, as Elise disappeared down the hall.

"What?"

"She does the right thing and dumps Chris because he's being a total jerkoff. But even though he's the jerk, she's the one without any luck in the school. And meanwhile Chris and Stephen and Ennis and Stacy and Tamara and the lot of them are running around lording their popularity over everyone. It's like the anointed can do no wrong or something. Like you and me and Elise and all the rest of us are just plebeians. Lowly parts of the masses who—"

"Wait!" I held up a hand. "I'm late."

She clamped her mouth shut, then her expression turned serious. "Maybe you're rushing into this."

I blinked. "You're kidding, right? You're the one who told Tamara that I'd do it!"

She looked appropriately chastised. "Well, yeah. But everyone knows I jump into things without thinking. It's practically my trademark. But *your* trademark is being smart. And I'm not sure you are. Being smart, I mean."

Okay, I have to admit that I did know what she meant. I'd been blinded by ego and lust and even though I didn't want to know it, I sort of did. Like Jenny said, I was smart. (Not smart enough as it turns out, which, frankly, was another nasty blow to my ego.)

"I haven't said yes yet," I pointed out. But that was only an excuse. We both knew I would. Ego and lust, remember?

"Yeah, but—" she began, but I was already gone, the common area floor slick under my sneakers as I sprinted down the hall.

The thing is, I'd had a thing for Stephen ever since my first week at Waterloo. I'd been a clueless freshman, unable to find my locker in the maze of hallways. I'd found Stephen, though. Plowed right into him, actually. He'd only been in school for two days (only in Texas for a week), but already, everyone knew that this sophomore was *hot*. The new football coach was already talking him up, and rumor was that Stephen would nail the varsity quarterback spot that was supposed to have been all tied up by Chris.

At any rate, even though he was so totally the man, he not only found my locker, he opened it, got my books, and walked me to class, asking me all sorts of questions about school and my friends and general life stuff. He was the first boy that hadn't treated me like I was a brainiac freak, and the whole experience had been dreamy. I think I've been a little bit in love ever since.

All of which meant that I was blind to basic questions. Like why Tamara and her gang had decided to anoint me instead of a blonder, prettier girl. Instead, I focused on my good fortune. A cheerleading notation on my transcript just when I needed it. And pizza with Stephen Wills, the boy I'd lusted quietly after since ninth grade.

Remember what I said about coincidences? I should have realized. I should have known.

But I didn't. Instead, I raced blindly over the well-waxed linoleum toward the double doors leading to the gym. I tried to slam through them, but hit something solid, then heard a yowl, followed by a sharp cry of "Shit!"

I cringed, pushed more carefully, and slid through the doorway to find myself face-to-face with Clayton Greene, his hand cupped over his nose and his face contorted in pain.

"Sorry!" I said, still cringing. "I didn't see you."

"I hope not. I'd be really pissed if you did that on purpose." He took his hand down and poked gingerly at his nose, wincing a little as he did. Thankfully, there wasn't any blood. I'd feel really bad if I'd injured him. Even though, honestly, I don't really like him.

Or, it's not that I don't *like* him. I do. Well, not like *that*, but you know. He's an okay guy. But he's always dogging me. We're in three classes together, plus he's on my newspaper staff. Actually, he's my assistant editor, which was Mrs. Shelby's doing, and the one thing I'll probably never forgive her for.

Clayton and I always seem to score within one point of each other on tests. It drives me crazy. And I know he wants to knock me off my valedictorian pedestal. And I'm so not letting that happen.

Still, I have to give him his props. I mean, he did stand up to Ennis earlier.

But the thing is, even though he's really smart, he's really stupid about some things. Like his clothes. Right then, for example, he was wearing a dark green flak jacket over a black T-shirt with some horrible looking monster design with fangs and a hatchet coming out of its head. I mean, gross!

Still, he's not a bad-looking guy. He's got really nice green eyes—but he wears glasses, not contacts, and the earpiece is usually attached with a glob of masking tape. And his hair is just a little bit too long, and always kind of shaggy. Like he's a friendly puppy. The kind of puppy that girls like Tamara like to kick. He's also got one tooth that sits kind of sideways. He gets teased about it, but I've always liked it. I think it makes him look like he's always smiling.

The point is he stands out. Which is fine if you're Johnny Depp. Which, of course, Clayton isn't.

Anyway, I was thinking all of that as I stood there watching him poke at his squashed nose. Then I realized that I was staring and raised a hand in a wave. "Sorry again," I said, "but I gotta go."

"Wait!" I hadn't gone but two steps. He took one long step and was right beside me. "I was waiting for you. I need to talk to you."

"Me? Why?" First Tamara, then Elise, and now Clayton. I was turning out to be quite the popular girl today.

"Are you really going to do it?"

"Do what?" I asked, squinting at him.

"Join the cheerleading squad?"

"How did you know about that?"

One skinny shoulder lifted in a shrug. Except it wasn't

as skinny as I remembered. Not that I was really paying attention or anything. I wasn't. Because I was too annoyed that he knew my personal business.

"Well?" I demanded.

"I hear things."

"So?"

"So, don't you think it's a little weird that suddenly Tamara's your new best friend?"

"What I think," I said snippily, "is that it's none of your business. And she's not my new best friend."

"That's even weirder," he said. "She's got no use for you for three years of high school. And then suddenly she's all hot for you to be a cheerleader? Give me a break."

"I don't recall asking your opinion," I said.

"Don't go." His voice was flat, serious. And he sounded truly concerned.

And because of that, I swallowed my first reaction, which was to tell him to mind his own business and go build a computer model of the solar system or something. Instead, I said, "What is up with you?"

"I can't—Just don't go. Okay? If you go out there tonight, I swear, you're going to regret it."

"Are you jealous?"

That threw him for a loop. "Jealous? Why would I be jealous?"

"Because you're breathing down my neck grade point–wise, and now I'm going to have a better range of extracurriculars on my transcript."

"You are a total freak," he said. "Even if that was true, why would I care about cheerleading?"

"Don't worry about me, Clayton Greene," I said. "Besides, you're right. I might regret it. I mean, if my grade point average slides a little because I have to go to cheer-leader practice, you might take my slot. So I'd think that you'd want me to join the squad."

Actually, that was an interesting point. So why on earth was he trying to discourage me?

He held out his hands in a gesture that sort of looked like surrender, but might have been exasperation. "Look, Beth. Just don't go, okay?"

Something in his eyes made me pause. Made me think that this really wasn't about grades. In fact, he looked so worked up about my plans for the afternoon that I almost caved in. I might have, too, if Stacy hadn't shown up.

But she did. And I didn't. And the rest, as they say, is history.

CHAPTER 6

"There you are!" Stacy said, exasperated. "Come on already! We've been waiting forever."

She didn't bother waiting for me to answer. She shot a nasty look in Clayton's direction, then took me by the arm and led me into the girls' locker room. And right before the door slammed behind us, I looked back and saw Clayton's face, his expression twisted, like he'd eaten something nasty and didn't have any place to spit it out.

I tried to shove the imprint of that expression out of my head as Stacy tugged me through the girls' locker room and out through the rear door that opened on the parking lot. "Um, shouldn't I change or something?" I asked, hooking a thumb toward the lockers that were disappearing behind the fast-shutting door.

She just looked at me, lifted an eyebrow, and kept on walking.

I hurried after. "I'm supposed to be coming to a practice, right? I can't do gymnastics in jeans."

"God, Beth," she said in a totally bored voice. "How is it you manage to make all those stellar grades without having anything remotely resembling a brain in your head?"

I probably would have turned around and gone home right then if we hadn't been halfway across the parking lot and in view of the bleachers. I couldn't make out faces yet, but I knew Stephen Wills was there. And so was Tamara and the rest of the squad. This was real. My transcript needed it. (And, yes, I even kind of wanted it.)

So I ignored Stacy's catty remarks and kept on.

Actual football games aren't played at our school. But like every other school in the country, we had our own practice field, complete with wooden bleachers under which many a girl has misplaced her virginity.

For the record, I should say that my virginity is perfectly intact. I mean, I've got a life planned. And I'm not really into the whole single parent idea. My parents have only been divorced for six months, and I can already tell that it sucks. (Well, actually dual parenting sucked, too. My parents really weren't cut out to procreate. From a philosophical standpoint, though, I guess I should be glad they did.)

To be honest, so far I hadn't gone out with any boy I'd be willing to let in my pants. Hand up my shirt, yes. I'm not a prude or a complete loser or anything. And—since I'm confessing all—I will say that I was eyeing the bleachers with more than a little thrill of anticipation. I mean, there's nothing wrong with fantasy, right? Fantasy that ended about third base and consisted of Stephen telling Tamara and the rest of the crowd to get lost.

Yeah, I thought. I could handle that kind of a fantasy just fine.

As we got closer, I could see Stephen sitting with Chris,

Ennis, Derek, and Nelson (yet more football players). Lisa, Joan, and Melissa—the other girls on the squad—were on the field practicing some jumps and lifts. And I've got to say, they rocked. I've been doing gymnastics as long as dance, and jumping into the kind of midair flips they were doing is a lot harder than it looks (and it looks pretty dang hard!).

As cheerleading squads go, Waterloo's is pretty small. Six girls total. The three on the field, Stacy, Tamara, and—apparently—me.

Most of the other high school squads in our division have more girls (this is the kind of fact you pick up as the editor of the paper). Last year, in fact, the squad had eight girls. The year before that, ten. Ladybell's been cutting the size of the team every year, even as she increases the size of the drill team. The drill team is pretty much like the Dallas Cowboy Cheerleaders. A whole kickline of bouncing, dancing girls. Apparently Ladybell was more into the dance end of things than the gymnastics end of things.

And considering she wasn't at my little audition, I had to figure I was right. Drill team, check. Cheerleading, not as much of a priority.

Apparently, my guide for the afternoon was Tamara. Who, I couldn't help but notice, wasn't practicing with the other girls. That's because she was curled up on Stephen's lap nibbling on his neck.

At least now my nausea wasn't just from nerves. I mean, *ick*.

Then again, maybe it was nerves. Or portents of doom. Or something.

Maybe Clayton was right. Maybe this was all a big mistake. After all, a stellar college application is one thing, but did I really want to spend the rest of the school year watching Tamara suck face with Stephen?

I did not, and I took a little break to run through every other extracurricular activity at Waterloo. I'd just about decided to take up the tuba (ha-ha) when I heard my name. I looked up and saw Stephen Wills walking toward me, a huge smile on his face and his arms out to his sides. Like he was going to grab me in a bear hug.

My palms started sweating and my stomach did little flip-flops, like it does before I stand up in class to read a paper or debate a point or something.

Yes, I know. Where was my pride? Tamara was *right there*. Probably smirking. And since Stephen obviously belonged to her—I could even see a red mark on his neck, where she'd obviously managed a hickey—my fantasies dissolved as fast as cotton candy dunked in water. But right then, I couldn't move. His eyes were on me, sucking me in, and I simply couldn't lift my feet. Stephen had cast a spell over me, and I couldn't do anything but stand there and then—slowly—walk toward him.

"Elizabeth!" I expected his outstretched arms to pull me in, so I was shocked when he stopped right in front of me, took my hand in his, and kissed it, just like a knight courting his lady.

I couldn't help glancing over toward Tamara. And even more, I couldn't help rubbing in my little victory by smiling at her, wide and bright.

She glared, looked away, then shot me one hate-filled look before rummaging through her purse for lip gloss.

As she started to freshen her makeup, I started to melt. Because Stephen was still holding my hand and the rising moon hung huge in the sky, cutting through the early evening darkness. Night came early now that we were already into November, and I was grateful. In the dark, I hoped, Stephen wouldn't be able to see me blush.

"You came," he said, in this supersexy voice. The kind that gets a guy a radio show. Or at least gets him the girl. "So it's settled. I'm so thrilled you agreed to join the squad."

"Ah . . . um . . ." I said, because I hadn't *officially* agreed to do anything yet. But as I looked into Stephen's excessively blue eyes, I couldn't for the life of me remember why I was hesitating. There was something weirdly hypnotic about his eyes. I felt a little like I was falling into them. Like I could get lost and happily spend eternity being a cheerleader to Stephen's football star. My lips felt all tingly, and I think I even leaned in.

But then he blinked.

He blinked, and so did I, and the fuzz in my head cleared and I realized that his pupils were as tiny as pinpricks. *But it was dark!* the science geek in my brain yelled. His pupils should be huge!

"Stephen," I said, my hand automatically going to his forehead. "Are you okay?"

He pushed my hand roughly away. "I'm fine."

"Your eyes. They're—"

He pressed a finger over his lips, and his eyes were on me again, and for the life of me, I couldn't remember why I was so concerned.

"I thought we could have a picnic. Just you and me."

"Oh." My loins quivered a little. No, *really*. I'm not sure I've ever in my life used the word "loins" before, but there was really no other way to describe it. They were *quivering*. And the fuzz in my brain was coming back. I knew I was supposed to be protesting about something, but I couldn't remember what. "But . . ." I trailed off, baffled and lust-filled.

"But?" he repeated.

I closed my eyes, exasperated with myself, and the fuzz in my brain melted. "I didn't realize we'd decided anything," I said. I looked back up at him. "I thought I was coming here to check out the squad. See if I fit in."

"Are you saying no?"

"I—" I tried to concentrate, but was having a hard time of it. I wished Jenny had come with me, because all of a sudden, my evening was feeling very surreal.

"If she doesn't want it, we can get someone else." Tamara, I realized, was standing right next to us. She brushed a finger over his neck, and I noticed that the hickey had completely faded. Not even the tiniest of red marks. "She's not the only one who can do this, you know," Tamara added, shooting me a hateful glare.

"Shut up, Tamara," Stephen said. For a second, I thought she was going to answer back. Then she spun on her heel and marched back toward the bleachers.

Stephen turned to me, the hardness melting away. "You will join the squad. Won't you?"

"I . . ." I trailed off, suddenly unsure.

"Excellent," he said, as if everything was decided. "You can start practices tomorrow." He nodded toward the field. "We've got beer, blankets. And there's no practice tonight. The girls are just fooling around." As if to illustrate the point, Melissa, Joan, and Lisa moved toward Ennis, Derek, and Nelson. I'd known that Melissa was dating Ennis (they'd been together since kindergarten) but Joan and Lisa's boy toys were a new one to me.

Stacy, of course, was parked on Chris's lap.

And that, I noticed, left Tamara the odd cheerleader out. No wonder she hated me.

My hesitation must have shown on my face, because he

took my hand again. "Come on, Elizabeth. It's your birthday. Let go a little."

If I were as smart as I think I am, warning bells would have gone off in my head. But the only bells that were sounding up there were happy chimes. *Stephen Wills knew my birthday!* How utterly amazing was that?

As it turned out, not nearly as amazing as the next thing he said. "I'm glad you came. I told Tamara if she couldn't get you on the squad, then to not bother getting anyone else."

"I—" I blinked, trying hard to process his words. "*You're* the one who told Tamara to put me on the squad?"

"Sure."

"But . . . but *why*?"

"I like you. I want you."

I should have protested. I should have listened to Clayton. Heck, I should have listened to my gut.

I should have said this was too weird and walked away.

But I couldn't. I couldn't move. I couldn't do anything. Because Stephen Wills was bending toward me, and when his lips touched mine, he captured me forever.

CHAPTER 7

Let's repeat that, because it's really important: when his lips touched mine, *he captured me forever.*

I know now that I should have said no. I should have gone home, called Jenny, rewatched the first season of *Buffy* on DVD. Something. *Anything.*

But Stephen Wills . . .

The Stephen Wills . . .

And he wanted to go out with me. *Me!* That perfect specimen of a guy, and he wanted to spend a few hours on a blanket drinking beer with me. (Yeah, I know. Pathetic, huh? But what can I say? I was awed. I was amazed. I was drop-dead, desperately in lust.)

And have I mentioned that his eyes are to die for?

No, really. They're to die for. And I mean that literally.

At the time, though, I wasn't thinking literally. Instead, I was all about metaphors. The coo of doves. The crash of waves. And awesome, blow-you-away, awe-inspiring fireworks.

Not that we started with fireworks. We started with beer. Which I pretended to drink. It's not that I never drink; it's just that I don't like beer. And I don't like being drunk. I tend to puke my guts up when I drink, and barf face is *so* not a good look for me.

As the others started passing around slices of pizza, Stephen led me by the hand back behind the bleachers to a little area with a blanket and an ice chest. Before we disappeared from view, I saw Tamara shoot me a look that could freeze hell, but I just smiled sweetly and tried to keep my knees from shaking.

Oh. My. God. Seduction city.

"Um, aren't we going to have some pizza?" How was that for smooth? I mean, is it any wonder that guys aren't throwing themselves at my feet? I'm such a clueless dork.

"We could have pizza," Stephen said. "But I'm wondering why you haven't touched your beer."

"Oh. Um." Well, heck. I was hoping he wouldn't notice that.

"Maybe you'd like this better," he said, then opened the ice chest and pulled out a bottle of tomato juice along with another, smaller bottle. Those, he followed up with a frosty bottle of vodka. "A little birdie told me you like Bloody Marys."

Okay, now that was *really* weird. Because I do like Bloody Marys. (Well, mostly I like the spiced tomato juice. The less vodka the better.)

"Oh. Well. Um. I don't know." After all, vodka is vodka. And I had a feeling I should be keeping my head on straight around Stephen Wills.

"Come on, Elizabeth," he teased, shaking the smaller bottle. "It's my secret recipe."

"Um. I . . . okay." And before you shout that I'm a total

pushover, my plan was to just, you know, sip it. I definitely wasn't going to drink it. And I very most definitely wasn't getting drunk. Because that would be stupid. And I'm not stupid.

Right? *Right.*

Or, as it turned out, wrong. But I didn't know that then. And the best-laid plans and all that . . .

Anyway, he mixed me the drink, then handed it to me. The tomato juice was a dark red, all the more in the dim light. I could smell the acidic tomatoeyness along with the vodka and spices. Something else, too, that I couldn't quite place, even though the scent seemed very familiar somehow.

Stephen made one for himself, too, and then he held out his glass. "To you," he said. "You're going to save our butts, you know."

"Our butts? What does the football team care if the cheerleaders win some competition?"

He just grinned. "Team spirit, Elizabeth. Now drink." I tasted mine tentatively, planning to only drink a little. I took one swallow, then another. Then another.

That's it, I told myself. *Stop now.*

My mouth, however, wasn't listening. Because the drink tasted fabulous. And it was making me feel . . . good? Not so much good as *comfortable.* Like maybe it wasn't so weird that Stephen wanted me under the bleachers. Like maybe I did have stuff to say and maybe I was pretty and maybe there wasn't any reason except for pure oversight that I'd gone three years being Miss Not At All Popular.

I don't know how, but when I looked down, Stephen was taking the empty glass from me, and I noticed that his glass was still full. "Slow down there, cowboy," he said. "That's powerful stuff."

I giggled. Honestly. I mean, if that's not a clue I wasn't entirely myself, I don't know what is. But I actually giggled. Worse, I didn't even mind.

"So, um, have you got anything to munch on?" Because I had the tiniest bit of presence of mind to know that I needed food. "Maybe some of that pizza?" I turned and looked toward the field. I couldn't see Tamara and crew anymore, but I could still remember the pizza. It sounded really good right then . . .

"Actually," Stephen said. "I've got something else to nibble on." He dropped his backpack to the ground, then pulled out a blanket.

"Oh." I waited for him to pull out sandwiches or something. Nothing. "Um, what?"

He sat, and then gestured for me to join him. "You."

Oh. My. God.

Let me repeat: Oh. My. God.

"I—" His laugh stopped me. "What?"

He took my hand and tugged me down beside him. "Don't tell me that innocent act you've got going is real."

I blinked at him, confused. Honestly, if I reacted this way every time some guy showed an interest in me, I'd be dateless and virginal until I was twenty-seven! And since that sounded like way too long to wait, I took a deep breath and tried to act like, well, like a cheerleader. I mean, if Tamara could suck his neck, the least I could do was not act like a scared little seventh-grader. Right? Right.

"Elizabeth?" he prodded, and I realized that in psyching myself up, I'd also completely shut myself down.

"Right. Sorry. I think the drink went to my head."

"Like I said," he said. "Innocent."

I bristled. "No. Well, okay, *yes*. But only from a practical standpoint. Philosophically, I'm not innocent at all." I have no idea what I meant by that, but it must have sounded good, because suddenly Stephen was laughing. And then he was moving. And then his leg brushed mine.

And then I started thinking that *practical* experience sounded a whole heck of a lot better than *philosophical* experience. Especially when the brush of his leg was burning a hole through my jeans and all I wanted to do was stop thinking and lose myself in this moment.

Because—just in case you forgot—*this moment* was a moment with Stephen Wills. *Stephen*. *Wills*. Under the bleachers. At night. With alcohol.

You do the math. I sure couldn't, since my ability to do math entirely evaporated when I felt his lips on my ear. "You taste good, Elizabeth," he said.

I made a small noise. Then I tried again. "Most people call me Beth."

"I'm not most people, now am I?"

No, he most definitely wasn't.

Warning bells clattered in my head. *What* was I thinking? I felt drunk, but I'd only had one Bloody Mary. Honestly, I hadn't realized I was such a lightweight.

"I don't feel so good," I said. And even as I spoke, I started feeling worse and worse.

"You're just light-headed," he said.

That was the truth.

"I'll make you feel better," he added. And then, before I could protest, I found myself curled up against him, and his palm was cupped over my breast, and I swear the only thought that went through my mind was that he was going to be sorely disappointed. Because I'm barely an A cup on the best of days. But when my boobs are all squished down in the sports bra I was wearing, there's really nothing up there at all. At least nothing any guy could get a grip on. Except . . .

Except now my head started swimming in a totally different way. Because Stephen had his hand on my chest and it felt really . . . nice. And even though I knew I should push him away—tell him to slow down and let me catch my breath—my mouth wasn't cooperating and the only sound that came from my lips was a little sigh.

What can I say? It felt really good. And that's only first base, right? Or maybe second. I'm not sure. But it wasn't like he was hitting a home run. I could get control of myself before he tried anything like that. Couldn't I?

A few seconds later, I wasn't so sure. Because his mouth was on mine, and it felt so soft and warm and nice. And *I* felt soft and warm and nice. All gooey and hot, like I could just melt right there.

I felt lost, hypnotized. Heck, I felt drunk. Drunk on lust and on Stephen's kisses. And then—*oh my gosh!*—he moved from my lips to my neck.

And when he started to nibble on my neck, this wave of warm gooeyness crashed over me. A wet warmth drenched my neck, and Stephen's little moans and slurping noises rang in my ears. The scent of copper filled my nose and my head started spinning even more. *Wow.* I'd never thought anything like this could happen to me. *Me.* Beth Frasier, Waterloo's resident smart girl.

And as I thought about that—how odd it was, I mean—it struck me that it really was weird. Why *would* Stephen want me? Why would any of them? Why was I so light-headed? And why couldn't I move my arms?

And why was my heart—which had been thumping so

hard and fast under Stephen's sweet ministrations—suddenly pounding in my ears at a decidedly slower tempo?

I didn't know, but all of a sudden I knew something was wrong. I tried to scream, really I did. But it was too late. Honestly, it was too late for anything at all.

You see, Stephen Wills killed me that night. The vampire's kiss, they call it. He sucked my soul in with those eyes, and then his teeth caught my neck and sucked me dry.

CHAPTER 8

Darkness.

Dark and damp and slightly cold.

I shifted, my limbs heavy and my eyelids even heavier. My blankets pressed down, trapping me in my bed, and I didn't have the energy to shove them aside.

For a split second I wondered why I was so fog-headed. And then I remembered. Bloody Marys.

And Stephen.

Stephen!

My eyes flew open as my muscles jerked back to life, trying, trying but failing to pull me upright.

The darkness was still there, and so was the damp. And even though my eyes were wide open, I couldn't see anything.

I opened my mouth and tasted the gritty, bitter earth.

I screamed, but the sound had nowhere to go.

And then, I think, I passed out.

CHAPTER 9

Okay. Rewind.

The next time I woke up, I was calmer. (Well, a little bit calmer.)

As much as I'd hoped that waking up inside the ground had been a really bad nightmare, I guess some tiny part of me had known it was all true. Just like some tiny part of me had known that Tamara inviting me on to the cheerleading squad was too good to be true. And that Stephen being interested in me *that way* was too good to be true.

I knew all those things were fiction, but I'd gone along with it. Why? Because I wanted my transcript to look good. (And, yes, because this was Stephen Wills we're talking about. And, yes, because his hand felt really good on my chest.) Anyway, lesson learned, right? The jocks and cheerleaders played one hell of a joke on good old Beth Frasier.

Well, screw them. If they thought they could get away with getting me drunk and then dumping me in some dirt pile—I don't think so! I had the power of the press at my fingertips, and I intended to use it to muckrake the whole mucked-up lot of them.

First, though, I needed to take a shower. The dirt had started to work its way into my clothes, and I was feeling really itchy. I wiggled my fingers and managed to shove my index finger up. First through semisolid dirt, and then—yes!—freedom!

Aaaaagh!

I yanked my hand back down into the cool dirt, cradling it under my chin. I couldn't see it—it's dark underground—but my finger felt like it was on fire. The pain was so intense, in fact, that I was woozy again. Like the way I'd felt when I sliced my thumb chopping cucumbers. And there was all that blood and my head started spinning and . . .

Get a grip!

I forced myself to calm down, then ordered myself to take deep breaths and count to ten the way I always did whenever I was pissed or scared. I took one—then immediately gagged and spat as dirt filled my mouth.

Okay. That was weird.

The good news was that the utter weirdness of the situation had taken my mind off my burning, throbbing finger. The bad news was that I'm pretty sure I'd been lying here underground—completely surrounded by dirt—and totally *not* breathing.

But that couldn't be right. Could it? I mean, people had to breathe. Of course, nobody would shove a person's body into the dirt unless—

Uh-oh.

I really didn't like the "unless," but I wasn't seeing a way around it. Slowly, I moved my noninjured hand through the dirt until I got it on my chest. I sat there, as still as death, and tried to find my heartbeat.

Nada.

Okay, this was bad. This was really, really bad. We'd gone way, way, way beyond bad dating horror stories here. This was Cryptkeeper territory.

My instinct was to sit bolt upright, plowing through the dirt and emerging from the earth like some scary monster in an old B movie. After that, I'd run home. I wanted my own bed. I wanted to see myself in the mirror. I wanted to IM Jenny and have her tell me this was all a really bad dream.

I even wanted to see my mom. And trust me, the way she's been since the divorce, that's saying a lot.

But I didn't. Chalk it up to my extreme self-control (or extreme terror—you pick), but I stayed put, my throbbing finger a reminder of what might happen to the rest of me if I clambered out of the earth.

I needed to think, and when you get right down to it, a dark, damp grave is a pretty good thinking spot. I mean, my only other option was hysteria. And I figured my chances for revenge were better if I was calm and rational. That's right. My self-control hinged on my overwhelming desire to get back at Stephen Wills, Tamara McKnight, and their little gaggle of idiot friends.

Which raised the first question for me to ponder: what exactly was I getting them back for? Burying me in the ground, sure. But considering the lack of heartbeat, I suspected there was more to it than that. I was dead . . . and yet, I wasn't.

Which raised another rather obvious question: what exactly was I now?

My first guess was a vampire. That fit, after all. Vampires are dead. But they're conscious (and considering the way my mind was whirring, I was most definitely conscious!). And sunlight burns them.

I eased my left hand closer to my face, slogging it through the dirt the whole time. I dug away a little hollow in front of my eyes, then moved my wristwatch in front of my face. My Timex lights up, but I couldn't move my right hand to push the button, and I was starting to feel frustrated all over again when I realized I could see the watch face just fine.

This, I figured, was both good and bad. Good in that I needed to see what time it was. Bad in that I apparently now had preternatural vision.

And, on the bad side of the equation, my watch showed that it was seven-fifteen in the morning. Daylight. And my finger—which I now realized I could see—was burned to a crisp.

Daylight. Burned flesh. Yup. All signs were definitely pointing to vampire.

Weirdly, however, I wasn't too freaked out. In fact, I was having a hard time concentrating at all. In fact, I was having trouble seeing the watch face anymore. And I realized almost offhandedly that the reason I couldn't see it was because my eyes were closed.

Exhaustion. Bone-tired exhaustion.

Why not? I thought. Vampires were supposed to sleep during the day.

And with that happy thought, my mind went blank, and I slept the sleep of the dead.

CHAPTER 10

In what I can only describe as a halfhearted attempt to keep my spirits up during this whole ordeal, I'm happy to report I've discovered that at least one of the Hollywood vampire rules applies—by the time I woke up again, my finger was completely healed.

From a scientific standpoint, that was fascinating. From a "gee, your life sucks" standpoint, one regenerative finger was hardly going to alter my overall mood.

And what exactly was that mood? Confused. Angry. Uncertain.

And terrified.

And, frankly, starting to get a little claustrophobic. I was a teensy bit hesitant about sticking my hand out of the ground again, so I checked my watch first. Well past six. The sun would have set almost an hour ago. So I sucked in my breath (figuratively only, because who wants to swallow dirt?) and shoved my fist straight up.

I waited a second, just in case my now-dead-and-undoubtedly-slower brain hadn't yet registered pain. But my fingers felt fine. I wiggled them, and as far as I could tell without actually looking, they were moving like they were supposed to.

I started shoving the dirt away, sitting up at the same time. It didn't take long. Apparently, they hadn't bothered to bury me too deeply or pack the dirt too tightly. I stood up, pausing a second to get my bearings. The vacant lot behind the school, the site of a now-demolished warehouse, the partial cinder block walls of which were now shielding me from traffic.

That, at least, was a good thing, as I really didn't want to be seen. I mean, I was covered in dirt. And while that might have been an okay look for Uma Thurman in *Kill Bill: Volume 2*, I didn't think it worked for me.

I stood still for only a second, then took off running. Stephen and the gang would be back for me—I was certain of that much. But I needed time to think, and I'd already learned the hard way that with Stephen around, my brain didn't fire on all thrusters.

The vacant lot was south of the school, and I circled around it, aiming toward the hike and bike trail that runs along the river. There's some cover there, what with all the trees and shrubs. And, fortunately, most of the joggers disappear once the sun goes down. Because who wants to run into a mugger on a dark jogging path?

Considering my new undead status, I wasn't too worried about being mugged. Or murdered, for that matter.

That gave me a nice little boost of confidence, but mostly, I just wanted to get home. So I raced down the path toward the pedestrian overpass, sprinted past the new Whole Foods and made a left onto Sixth Street, raced a few more blocks, then turned right at Blanco. This is not exactly a short distance, but I wasn't even winded. Chalk one up for vampirism. I never had to do Pilates again!

Our house is on a street with lots of old, refurbished houses. I've always thought the neighborhood was cool. Now it looked eerily *'Salem's Lot*–ish. My parents bought it when I was ten and they were happy. At the time, the place was a complete dump. A two-bedroom, one-bath bungalow that cost, as my dad said, "more money than God has."

About three years ago they started remodeling. That was fun (not). The dust that hung in the air wasn't nearly as thick as the tension between them.

When the remodel was finally finished earlier this year, we celebrated by going to Jeffries and having this really fabulous dinner. My parents actually talked and laughed and for the first time I didn't feel like someone was standing on my chest. I remember falling asleep thinking about my very own bathroom, my much bigger bedroom, and my newly amicable mom and dad.

Life was good.

For about one week. Then the fighting started again. Or, at least, it started when they were home together, which was pretty close to never. And the ice-cold tension. And the mean looks and the slamming doors and, honestly, you would have thought that I was the grown-up!

Even so, I never expected the D word. It came, though. About one month after the remodel was finished, they called me into the living room and told me that my dad was moving out. By the next morning he was gone.

"Don't worry," they both said to me. "We both still love you very much. Nothing's going to change that."

And you know what? They were right. I hardly saw either of them before the divorce, and when I did, they were grumpy and stressed. Now I still hardly see them. When I do, they're grumpy and stressed.

I had a feeling I was coming home to a *major* grump session. I mean, I've never once stayed out all night. So I was certain that today my mom would be sitting at the kitchen table, editing a legal brief, chewing out some underling on her cell phone, and waiting to lay into me.

The thing is, I didn't want Mom to see me like this. Looking like I crawled out of a grave, I mean. So I planned to sneak in, scrub down in my bathroom, then come in through the kitchen like usual.

Fortunately, luck was on my side, because my bedroom window was open just a crack. I'm supposed to keep a nail in the window so that it can't be opened from the outside. But I'm always forgetting to do that. Mom says I'm risking our lives; that anyone can break in. At the moment, that was good news for me.

I pulled the screen off and tossed it aside. Then I pushed the sash all the way up. The window is only about waist high, so all I really needed to do was lean in, then scootch until my hips and legs were inside, too. If I was lucky, I'd manage all that quietly. If I was unlucky, my mom would hear the thud as I landed on the hardwood floor.

What I hadn't counted on was being really, really, *really* unlucky. As in, the second I pulled myself up and over, I hit a solid wall of electrified nothing. I yelped in surprise and pain as a jolt of something ripped through me, and I found myself flying backward through the air.

What the heck?

For just an instant, I wondered if Mom had installed some sort of alarm system. Except that unless someone had invented a *Star Trek*–type force field for, you know, home security, I was thinking that wasn't really too likely.

As I sat there on my rump, I finally figured out the real reason—I didn't have an invitation.

Ha! you're probably saying. *That's stupid. You live there. You don't need an invitation.* Yeah, well, that's only sort of true. Since I was dead, I no longer *lived* there. And that meant I could only go in if I was invited. And that meant only one thing—

I was going to have to knock on the door and show my filthy, dirt-covered self to my mom.

Great.

I spent a few seconds thinking up a plausible excuse (I decided on a half-truth: my jerk of a date took me out, slipped me a roofie, and I woke up in a pile of dirt), then marched to the front porch. A couple of deep breaths for the sake of courage, and then I knocked.

No answer.

Okay. Fine. I rang the doorbell. Waited. No answer.

I frowned and pounded. You guessed it—no answer. My mother wasn't home. I was missing, and she wasn't home. What was wrong with *that* picture?

Unless she'd gone to my dad's so that they could commiserate together? But since my cell phone (and my purse for that matter) was missing, I couldn't call, and I didn't want to talk to the neighbors looking like I did. If Mom was with Daddy, he'd tell her to come back here and wait for me. And if she'd gone to the police, they'd tell her the same thing.

So I just needed to wait. A plan that I wasn't terribly crazy about, but what choice did I have?

Since our garage is detached and in the back of the house, I moved to the backyard, parked myself on the porch, and waited.

Two hours later—*two freaking hours!*—she pulled into

the garage, apparently not noticing me standing and waving from the porch. She came out the side door a second later, her heels clicking on the flagstone path.

When she reached the first step up to the porch, she finally noticed me. "Beth! Darling, what are you doing outside?" Her nose wrinkled and she looked me up and down. "And what on earth have you been up to?"

I opened my mouth to answer, but couldn't quite find the words. This really wasn't the reception I'd been expecting. I'd been *missing* here, folks. Face-on-the-milk-carton territory. Hello? Why wasn't she throwing her arms around me and crying in relief?

I squinted at her, trying to see even a hint of tears in her eyes, but she was already past me and had her key in the door. "I'm so sorry I wasn't home last night. I can't believe I had to fly to Dallas for that damn deposition." She turned and smiled at me. "But I totally discredited their witness. It was a beautiful thing."

I blinked, realizing that she hadn't even realized I'd been gone. Then I stood there on the stoop, unable to follow her inside. She dropped her briefcase in a kitchen chair, then turned and gestured impatiently in my direction. "Well, don't just stand there. Come inside so that we're not inviting every bug in to join us."

Not every bug, I thought. Just me.

And then I accepted the invitation and went inside.

CHAPTER 11

I've always done some of my best thinking in the shower, and right then I had a lot of thinking to do. So I avoided any more of my mom's wrath and headed straight for my bathroom. I didn't even bother adjusting the water temperature, either. Just turned the hot on full blast. And you know what? It felt *wonderful*.

Until I remembered that I was being pummeled with scalding hot water. I *should* be screaming in pain. I *should* be leaping out of the shower and desperately trying to switch the water to cold.

I wasn't. Because, hey, I wasn't human anymore.

This being dead thing really was going to take some getting used to.

The thing is, I didn't want to get used to it. I wanted my life back, and I wasn't even certain if that was possible. I mean, dead is dead, right?

Except that dead isn't anywhere near as dead as I thought it was, because I was standing in my shower, massaging

Aveda's rosemary mint shampoo into my hair. This was new territory, and I wasn't even sure how to begin, much less *where* to begin.

I needed answers. I needed a plan. I needed Obi-Wan or Gandalf or Giles—*some* mentor type dude who'd show me the ropes and tell me how to deal. And, more important, how to get my life back. If I even could get my life back.

But most important of all, I wanted to find Stephen Wills. Find him, and get back at him.

I just wasn't sure how.

And even if I shoved revenge aside . . . how was I going to manage going to class? If my academics nose-dived now, Tisch would never—

Oh.

That's when it hit me. And, yes, I probably should have put it all together already, but forgive me for being a little freaked out. But right then I realized exactly what the situation was: *I was dead*.

Dead. Kaput. Out of the game.

I wasn't going to Tisch. I wasn't even going down the street to the University of Texas.

Yeah, I was dead and all. But right then, I realized that my life was *really* over—a revelation that even my incredibly long shower couldn't change. Still, by the time I got out, I was dirt-free and smelled good.

I stood there, wrapped in a towel, and leaned in close to the mirror to brush my teeth and search for fangs. None. Which was interesting in a what-do-I-do-with-this-information-now sort of way.

But what was *really* interesting was the fact that I could see my teeth perfectly well. So at least one bit of vampire lore was a complete crock—my reflection was showing up just fine.

That little fact actually made me feel a tiny bit better, and I started brushing my fang-less mouth with renewed vigor. I mean, we're talking basic laws of physics here. Yes, I'd been turned into a walking, talking creature of the night, but I could accept that (kinda sorta). But what would *completely* throw me for a loop was if the whole world started working wrong.

Honestly, the kinds of myths that Hollywood foists on an unsuspecting public . . . Of course, when *I'm* a famous director/screenwriter/producer, I'll only produce movies of the highest quality. True movies, that really speak to the human condition and—

I stopped brushing, once again remembering that I wouldn't be going to film school. And if I did manage to make it in Hollywood, all my films were going to be shot at night.

Did I mention that Stephen Wills was on my shit list?

Now clean, I headed into my bedroom and turned on my computer. I think best when I'm making lists, and that's what I was going to do: make a What Do I Do Now That I'm Dead? list.

I was about to pull up a blank document when the IM box popped up.

SoNotMissTexas: U there?
EdInChief: Am now.
SoNotMissTexas: WHERE hve u been? Worried!!
EdInChief: Have lots to tell you. Later.

No way was I keeping my vampiness from my best friend. But at the same time, I didn't think that IM'ing the news that I was now undead was the best way to handle the situation.

SoNotMissTexas: ?????????????
EdInChief: What?
SoNotMissTexas: Hello?????? WHAT HAPPENED? Waited
    4 you at school today. You never showed. So TELL
    ME ALREADY. (BTW, the Watcher ragged on Chris
    and Ennis! Check it out.)
EdInChief: Later
SoNotMissTexas: Which? Blog or telling moi?
EdInChief: Both
SoNotMissTexas: Am coming over . . .
EdInChief: LATER
SoNotMissTexas: See ya in thirty.

And she broke the connection. Honestly, this really
wasn't my day.

I decided not to worry about Jenny. Instead, I stared at
my computer screen and tried to come up with a brilliant
plan.

So far, nothing.

I clicked over to the *Waterloo Watch* blog and read what
Jenny had written, figuring it might inspire me.

The Watcher has it on good authority that our own be-
loved (ha-ha) tailback, Ennis Walker, is suffering from
some sort of severe neurological disorder. No, seriously!
Dozens of witnesses in the caf on Monday watched as
he and tag-along linebacker, Chris Freytag, razzed on a
student who was doing nothing more than minding his
own business. Once again, C&E proved that homopho-
bia is alive and well at Waterloo High (I mean, grow up,
you guys!).

Anyway, all of these witnesses saw E's face twitch and
shift and look even grosser than normal (let's face it, E is

not winning Mr. America anytime soon). Clearly some sort of musculature disorder, the Watcher thinks. And now the Watcher is wondering: is this disorder the reason why E is never in morning classes? Has he been given some sort of medical excuse? Because, you know, how can a guy who skips his early classes still make good enough grades to stay on the football team?

Hmmm.

Check back for all the dirt. And don't forget, the Watcher watches so you don't have to!

CHAPTER 12

Even though Jenny's blog entry totally rocked—a neurological disorder! I loved it!—the blog had not inspired any revenge ideas, which meant I was right back where I started.

I swiveled in my desk chair and glanced out my bedroom door. I have a *great* desk chair. My parents gave me an Office Depot gift card after breaking the divorce news, and I bought the best. It swivels and has rollers and I can move anywhere in my bedroom on it. Right then, I used my toes to push me and my chair closer to the door so I could see down the hall and into the kitchen.

I didn't see my mom, but I saw her shadow, moving around in there, probably making a snack or getting some coffee as she prepared to stay up working on briefs again. Have I mentioned my mom's a lawyer? Maybe she could sue Stephen for me. That was something, right? Of course, I'd have to tell her what happened, but maybe I ought to do that anyway. After all, don't moms want to know this kind of stuff? When their kids are made undead, I mean?

I blinked and realized that even though my stomach was all knotted up and my throat felt thick, I wasn't actually crying. Another side effect of vampiness. I couldn't even wallow in a good cry.

And as clueless and absent as my mom is, right then I wanted her anyway. I wanted her to hug me and tell me it was gonna be all right. And I wanted her to tell me that she'd help me figure out a way to get back at Stephen Wills. I needed help. As much as I hated to admit it, I clearly couldn't figure this one out on my own.

I got up and went into the kitchen. I wasn't entirely sure *how* I was going to tell her (I mean, we never even officially had *the* talk). But I figured I'd wing it.

In the kitchen, I found mom hunched over the table, LexisNexis and Westlaw printouts spread out all around her, and a legal brief so edited with red pen that it looked like someone had opened a vein and bled on it.

Honestly, the thought made me a little hungry.

She looked up sharply when I walked in. "You look better. More." She held out her cup. I poured.

"Um, Mom?"

"Damn it!"

I jumped back. "What?"

She looked up as if she'd totally forgotten I was there. "These damn first years. Why do they let them out of law school if they don't even have a basic grasp of the law? Not to mention how to write a sentence." She pointed her pen at me. "If you ever give a partner a brief this sloppy, you will never hear the end of it from me."

"No worries," I said, since I never intended to turn any

legal briefs in to anybody. "Um, Mom? There's, uh, something I want to talk to you about."

She looked up again, and I saw irritation in her eyes. Then I guess she remembered that at home she's not just a lawyer, because the irritation vanished and she smiled. I had the impression for a second that her face was going to crack (my mom doesn't smile a lot), but at least she was looking at me.

"Right. Yeah. Well. You see, the thing is that I—"

"Elizabeth, I know what this is about."

"You do?" She couldn't possibly.

"I do, and I'm sorry." She got up and moved across the kitchen for her purse. "I can't believe I had to go out of town on your birthday."

I blinked. Considering everything that had happened, my birthday wasn't exactly a priority. Still, she had a point. It was my *sixteenth* birthday. She was totally supposed to have been home.

"I got you this, though." She held out an envelope. I took it and opened it. Inside I found a Barnes & Noble gift card for two hundred dollars. The credit card receipt was in there, too. I recognized my mom's secretary's name. So much for the personal touch.

"I know how much you love your books. Forgive me?"

I nodded, numb. "Sure. Thanks. This is great."

"Was that it?" she asked. "What you wanted to talk about? I have to file this brief tomorrow and it's in terrible shape."

"Sure," I said, nodding. "That's all it was." And, yeah, maybe I'm being a little overly sensitive, but I figured if my mom couldn't take ten minutes to buy me a birthday present herself, I really didn't expect she could find the time to deal with any more of my problems.

I blinked again, suddenly really glad about that whole no-crying thing.

"Anything else?" She tapped her pen on the brief. Apparently, I was cramping her style.

"No. I'll just get something to drink." All of a sudden, I was incredibly thirsty. I mean *ravenously* thirsty.

Mom grunted and went back to her brief as I opened the refrigerator and pulled out a jug of milk. I poured a tall glass and then took a big gulp. It was cool, refreshing . . . and made me completely sick!

My stomach cramped worse than I've ever felt during my time of the month. I dropped the glass and it shattered on the wooden floor, sending milk and shards flying everywhere. I didn't care, I was on my knees, hunched over, vomiting my guts up.

The pain didn't let up until every tiny bit of milk had been purged, and then I leaned back against the cabinet and tried not to totally freak out.

"Beth! Are you sick?"

Hello? This is the reasoning ability of one of the greatest legal minds in the country? "Um, yeah."

"Well, then off to bed." She got up and patted my shoulder. "Go on, now. If you're sick, you need sleep."

Escape was more like it, and I was just about to go hide out in my room when the phone rang. I snatched it up out of habit, then immediately froze when I heard the voice on the other end. "Elizabeth? Good. You made it home."

"Stephen." I glanced at my mom and refrained from screaming at him like a raving lunatic. It wasn't easy, though. I wanted to move out of the kitchen, but the kitchen phone is the old-fashioned kind, and I was tethered there by a yellow curlicue cord.

"How are you adjusting?" His tone was completely blah,

like he was talking about a change in my schedule, rather than a change in my life.

"Oh, just peachy," I said, gritting my teeth and trying to smile casually at my mom.

"Glad to hear it. Listen, I need you at the bleachers tomorrow at sundown." Totally normal. Like nothing bad had happened at all. Was this guy mental?

"That sounds like oodles of fun, Stephen. But I think I'll be busy." I was using my sickly sweet voice. The one that I use when I want people to know I think they're a raving idiot. "In fact, I'm busy now. Gotta go. Bye."

"Wait."

I was about to hang up when his voice came through. So loud, in fact, that my mom looked up, too. I smiled sheepishly and shoved the phone back against my ear.

"What?"

"I don't think you understand," he said, all of that false nice-boy tone now gone. "I made you. When I say jump, you ask how high."

"Excuse me?"

"You can try it the other way, but I don't think you'll like the results. Bad things happen to vampires who don't follow their master's orders."

I opened my mouth to say something, but nothing came out. *Master*. Stephen Wills was my *master*?

Suddenly, I really wanted another shower.

"So, I'll ask again. Where are you going to be at sundown tomorrow, Elizabeth?"

"The bleachers," I said. "Thanks so much for the invitation."

As comebacks went, it was pretty lame, but he laughed. "You're going to work out just fine," he said. "And I think you'll even like it, once you get used to it."

"Don't bet on it."

"Tomorrow," he said. Then he hung up. I stood there a second, staring at the phone.

What the freaking hell just happened?

I mean, this was getting worse and worse by the minute! Stephen didn't pick me to be on the cheerleading squad! He didn't even pick me to be his date!

He didn't even really *want* a date. He just wanted a minion.

How's that for sick irony? The creep who killed me was now the head vampire in my personal vampire hierarchy. And the rules of my new little community of fiends— excuse me, *friends*—required me to do his bidding.

He ruined my life, screwed up my plans for college, and completely botched my birthday. And *now* he expects me to lift a finger just because he says so?

Um, I don't think so.

Stephen Wills was dead meat. Literally and figuratively. Him, his idiot jock cohorts, and those uber-bitches, Tamara McKnight and Stacy Plunkett.

What's that saying? Hell hath no fury like a woman scorned? Maybe so. But believe me, it's also true that hell hath no fury like a valedictorian screwed out of a chance to go to college.

Trust me on that.

They were going down, and somehow I was getting my life back.

I didn't know how exactly, but I wasn't worried. I'm smart, remember? And as it turns out, I had all the time in the world.

CHAPTER 13

According to Khan, revenge is a dish best served cold. That's all good and well, but it's really, really hard to plot revenge when you're starving to death. Or not to death, but . . .

Oh, to heck with it. I was hungry! More specifically, I was thirsty. And you can probably guess what I was craving.

I was back in my room; I couldn't help but glance toward the kitchen. Only this time it wasn't the refrigerator I was thinking about. It was my moth—

No, no, no, no, no!

No way was I drinking my mom's blood! For that matter, no way was I drinking anyone's blood! I mean, ick!

Except, apparently, I had to eat.

I tried to think of what to do, but the only thing that came to mind was *Interview with the Vampire* and the whole rat's blood–drinking thing.

I thought about that, but didn't much like the idea.

For one, where was I supposed to find a rat? If there

were any living near my house, believe me when I say I *really* didn't want to know about it.

For another, how was I supposed to get the blood out of the rat? I sure as heck wasn't biting it. I mean, those things carry all sorts of diseases! And their fur is . . . well, yuck! And I honestly didn't think I was up to slicing its little throat. I don't like rats, but that's just plain mean! Honestly, I'd rather starve to death!

Except I wouldn't. Not really.

And then it hit me—what about a blood bank?

Since that seemed like a half-decent idea, I shut my door and grabbed up my phone. I'm not supposed to call information ("Twenty-five cents per call! You can use the phone book, young lady!"), but I figured this was an extenuating circumstance.

As it turned out, though, the blood bank was closed. I guess that was probably just as well. I mean, what was I going to tell them? That I had a savings account and wanted to make a withdrawal? That I needed a bag of blood for a school project? That I wanted to make a hemoglobin milksha—

Wait a second.

I mentally reran my thoughts, then realized that I *did* have an option. Not a perfect option, but I thought it would work.

Especially if I played the birthday card.

CHAPTER 14

As soon as I hung up with my dad, I called Jenny's cell phone. "Where are you?"

"I'll be there in five. I had to beg for the car. It was a whole big production. Honestly, I should join the drama club."

I waited for her to stop rambling. "Do me a favor?"

"Sure."

"Before you come, swing by the hospital. My dad's going to leave something for me at the information counter in Admitting." My father the doctor is desperate for his darling daughter to follow in his footsteps, so I'd been pretty sure that he'd jump when I said "science project." And I'd been right. I didn't even have to mention the forgotten birthday, which was just as well since I really didn't need the drama.

"Swing by?" Jenny squealed. "That's like totally out of my way."

"It's really important."

She sighed.

"Come on, Jen. I'd get it myself, but no one gave me a car for my birthday. And I'm not exactly in my mom's good graces right now. You know?"

"Fine. Whatever." She readjusted her arrival time to thirty minutes. "But you still have to tell me *everything*."

She walked into my bedroom twenty-two minutes later, swearing she didn't break any traffic laws. I didn't care if she'd broken them all. I'd spent the last twenty-two minutes willing myself not to jump the mom-meal in the kitchen. I mean, I didn't want to, but this craving was so beyond my desperate need for M&M'S during my period that I wasn't really sure I could control it.

"I met your mom on the way in," she said. "She told me to tell you that the brief was a piece of crap and she was going back to the office and that she'd probably be there all night and she'd see you tomorrow." She rattled that off and then drew in a deep breath. "God, your mom is a scary, scary lady!"

I agreed wholeheartedly, but I didn't say anything. I was too focused on the cooler she had in her hand. She caught me looking and passed it to me. "So what is this, anyway?"

I was too thirsty to talk. I just reached out and grabbed the cooler, then bolted into my bathroom, slamming the door behind me. I yanked the lid off and there, nestled in a bunch of ice packs, I found ambrosia: twelve pint bags of blood.

I took back every mean thing I ever said about my dad, then grabbed up one of the bags. I looked around for my razor to make a slice in the plastic, then realized I didn't need it. That tingling feeling in my mouth was caused by sprouting fangs. How convenient. Gross, but convenient. And without any more ado, I closed my mouth over the plastic, punched my teeth through, and sucked.

I'd drained the packet and was about to bite into a second one when Jenny barged in. "I can't wait! I have to hear about Steph—" She stopped and stared. I wished I'd remembered to lock the door. "Oh. My. God."

She backed out of the bathroom, then turned and ran. I managed to come down off my little wave of satiated satisfaction long enough to realize that this was A Bad Thing.

I tossed the second bag into the sink and tore after her. She'd gotten a decent head start, though, and was already through the kitchen and fumbling with the lock on the back door.

"Jenny, wait!"

"Screw that!" She managed to flip the lock and pulled the door open.

"Jenny! It's not what it—" I shut up, because it was *exactly* what it seemed to be.

She barreled down the steps, and I barreled right along behind her. Barreled right over her, actually, because I was faster than I was used to and not doing too great a job at judging distances and stuff. She fell and I fell on top of her.

She screamed and held her fingers like a cross. "No! Beth! I'm your best friend! Please don't kill me!"

"I'm not going to kill you!" I said, but I barely got the words out before I found myself being pulled off her by the back of my collar. Then someone tossed me back down and loomed over me *with a huge freaking wooden stake*!

I screamed and tried to roll away, but there was nowhere to go, what with Jenny on one side and our huge oak tree on the other. And here comes Blade swooshing down on me and leading with the stake, and all the while I'm tossing my arms up to protect myself and thinking that this is it. Now I really *will* be dead. Dead dead. Not undead.

Except he didn't make it to my heart. He didn't even make it past my arms. Because Jenny threw herself across me and yelled, "You just leave her alone! Leave. Her. Alone."

"But she's a vampire!" came the answer, and *I knew that voice*!

"Clayton?"

"Don't talk to me, evil spawn of Satan!"

"Hey!" Jenny said. "You take that back!"

"I am *not* the spawn of Satan!" I mean, I may not think my parents are the greatest, but they're not that bad!

"I told you not to go out there," Clayton said. "I *warned* you!"

"You knew?" I tried to sit up, but with Jenny sprawled protectively across my chest, I couldn't move.

He ignored me, instead, kicking at Jenny's thighs. "Get out of the way, Jenny! She's not your friend anymore. Once she drinks, she's doomed forever."

"She *is* my friend!"

"Then why were you running?"

I'm actually glad he asked that. I mean, I was thrilled Jenny had saved me from the stake and all, but I wasn't entirely sure why she had.

"I was . . . freaked out," Jenny said. "Yeah. Really freaked out. I mean, you would be, too, right?"

"Yeah," Clayton said. He gestured with the stake. "And then I'd get over it and do what needed to be done."

Honestly, I felt a little stupid just lying there, but I wasn't sure what else to do. Run and he might catch me. And, also, I remembered the way I felt when I'd been so thirsty. Around my mom, I mean. What if I felt that same way when I got angry or scared or really riled up in a fight? I mean, even though Clayton was really pissing me off, I didn't want to bite him.

At any rate, I doubted Jenny would let me up. Right then she was telling Clayton in the most stringent of tones that she wasn't some "narrow-minded sycophant who abandons a friend simply because she happens to be part of a misunderstood minority!"

"Misunderstood minority?" he parroted. "She tried to suck your blood!"

"I did not!" I said.

"Shut up, you lying undead animal!"

"Hey!" Now he was starting to hurt my feelings!

"Leave her alone!" Jenny said. "It's not her fault. She didn't do this to herself." She twisted around to look at me. "Did you?"

I rolled my eyes. "Stephen The-Big-Jerk Wills."

"See?" Jenny said, turning back to Clayton.

"Why are you defending her? She tried to kill you!"

"No, I—"

"She did *not*."

"Yeah? Then how come you were running? How come there's blood all over her mouth?"

"There's not any on my neck," Jenny shot back. "Is there, Sherlock?"

"Well . . ."

"Would you two shut up?" I said. "I was drinking from hospital bags. No way would I hurt Jenny! Like she said, she ran because she was freaked. I mean, I can understand that. I'm freaked, too."

He stepped back, his stake lowering just a bit. "So, you didn't bite her?"

"I told you. No."

"And you haven't bitten *anyone*?"

"For the umpteenth time, *no*."

He looked at Jenny. "Really?"

"Honest. I brought blood when I came over." She made a face. "I didn't *know* it was blood, but she drank it and I saw, and—"

"—that's when you so rudely interrupted," I finished.

"Well, okay." He slid the stake into a pocket and held a hand out for Jenny. "Get up, then."

"Like hell."

"I'm not going to stake her," he said wearily. "If she hasn't drunk from a person yet, there's still hope."

At that, I perked up. "There is? What are you talking about? And how do you know all this stuff anyway?"

Clayton nodded toward my still-open back door. "Let's go inside," he said. "And I'll tell you everything."

CHAPTER 15

"You've, um, got a little, um . . ." Clayton pointed to his cheek. "Um, some . . . stuff. Right there."

We were sitting around the table, Jenny protectively pacing behind me, and Clayton across from me. I grabbed a napkin off the table and dabbed at my mouth. "Better?"

"Better?" Jenny repeated, her voice rising. "Beth, you were drinking blood! And your teeth were pointed!"

"Um, yeah." I kind of thought we were past that. I mean, wasn't that the cause of the freak-out in the first place? Wasn't that why Clayton had tried to kill me? Had my friend really *just* clued in here? And besides, my teeth weren't pointed anymore.

"Why?" she asked, sliding into the chair at the head of the table.

I exchanged glances with Clayton. "Vampire," I said. "Remember? Undead. All those names he called me."

"Sorry 'bout that," he said. Then he smiled. And it was

a *really* nice smile. For a guy who'd tried to kill me a few minutes earlier, he was being awfully nice now.

Who knows? Maybe I misjudged him. Maybe Clayton's not just out to push me off my GPA throne. I mean, I'd sure as heck been wrong about Stephen. So maybe I'd been wrong about Clayton, too.

"Hello?" Jenny said, waving a hand. "You wanna tell me *how*? How could you be at school one day, perfectly normal. And then be . . ." She trailed off, her hand floating up and down as she gestured to me. *"This."*

"Stephen Wills," Clayton said. "She already said."

Jenny's brow furrowed, like she was trying to figure out a really hard algebra problem. "So, Stephen's the one who, um . . ."

"Made me?" I suggested.

"Well, yeah." And then she started laughing, which wasn't the reaction I was expecting.

"Jenny!"

"Sorry. I never thought I'd hear anyone say that Stephen Wills and you made it."

"Ha-ha. You're a real comedian, you know that?"

"Honestly! I'm sorry!" She looked contrite, so I forgave her. "It's just, you know, funny."

I made a face but decided not to press the point. Instead, I turned to Clayton "How did *you* know?" I demanded. "And why did you come here? And why did you say there's still hope?"

He took one of those really deep breaths, then slipped off his flak jacket. He had on a black T-shirt and I noticed that his arms were actually quite buff. Not at all the skinny Clayton I remembered from seventh grade. "I'll tell you," he said, taking the stake out of his pocket and setting it on the kitchen table. "But I want to hear your story first. All the details. Who was there. What they said. What they did. Everything you remember."

"And about the blood," Jenny said. "I'm like totally jazzed that you didn't bite me and all, but isn't that what vamps do? So why were you sucking plastic?"

I made a face that I hoped conveyed just how unpleasant the idea of taking a bite out of a person was. Tempting, but definitely unpleasant.

At any rate, I told them. The whole thing. Lust and Bloody Marys and bites and all. Well, maybe not the lust part. I'd fill Jenny in on those details later, but I was *so* not talking about my love life in front of Clayton. *That* was not part of the bargain!

Anyway, I described waking up in the dirt, and burning my finger, and finally making it home only to be trapped outside, and then finally, finally getting inside.

"But then I got so thirsty," I finished, "that I was on the verge of biting my mom. But I couldn't do that. I mean, you know," I said, looking at Jenny.

She nodded. There are at least a million reasons why it would be bad form for the vampire Beth to bite her mom. Jenny understood this. That is one of the reasons that we are such good friends.

"So I called my dad and asked him for the blood."

Her eyes widened. "Your dad knows you're a vampire and he didn't tell you to go ahead and bite your mom?"

"Ha-ha," I said. "And he doesn't have a clue. I told him I was doing a science project and I needed it right away."

"Ah," Jenny said, as if that explained everything. Which, of course, it did. Then she shifted, eyeing me kind of sideways.

"What?" I asked.

"So, like, did it taste good?"

I glanced toward my bathroom and the bag of blood still in the sink. *Oh yeah. It tasted like heaven.*

I had a feeling that wasn't the answer Jenny wanted, though. Plus, I saw Clayton looking at me all squinty-eyed. So I sat up a little straighter, then lifted a shoulder, trying for casual. "It didn't make me gag."

"You're not gonna want *fresh* blood anytime soon are you?"

Aha. "God, Jenny! I already told you guys! I'm not going to bite your neck and suck your blood! The idea is totally repulsive! Now will you get with the program? I've got a lot of stuff to figure out here."

They stared at me for a second, probably not quite sure if I was really a kinder, gentler vampire. Actually, I wasn't sure myself. I'd never in a million years tell Jenny (and I sure wouldn't tell Clayton!), but the truth was that the idea of fresh, flowing blood did sound sort of . . . I mean . . . well . . . let's just say it made my teeth feel all tingly again. I kept my mouth firmly closed and stared at Jenny, daring her to call me a liar.

She didn't. (Thank goodness.) Instead, she turned to Clayton. "So what's the deal? Why is there hope? Can she be turned back?"

I leaned forward. "Can I?"

He leaned back in his chair and cocked his head. He looked very comfortable, very cocky, and, frankly, very cute. "Maybe," he said.

The glow of cuteness faded. "Maybe?" I repeated. "Maybe doesn't do me any good."

He leaned forward, propping his elbows on the table. "Look, Beth, it's not like I've got a lot of experience with this. But I do know that you're in sort of a nether-region, at least until you draw living blood."

I squinted at him, something tickling my memory. "And you know this how?"

He shrugged and didn't quite look at me. "I just do."

"Oh, no," I said, shaking my head. I stood up, then started pacing my kitchen. "Just because you've seen a dozen or so vampire movies, you are not some sort of vampire expert."

"I never said I was."

"Oh." I frowned. "Well, then why do you think that I'm not really a vampire until I kill?"

"First of all, I never said you weren't a vampire. And second of all, I never said you had to kill." He looked at me seriously. "Honestly, Beth, your attention to detail—"

"My details are just fine," I interrupted. "For example, I remember the little detail about how you didn't stop me from going with Stacy! I mean, you knew they were going to do this to me, and you let me go anyway. Care to explain *that* little detail?"

He looked a little sheepish, but the expression faded with a cocky lift of his chin. "I tried to warn you, but you went anyway."

"Well, yeah! But I thought I was just joining the cheerleading squad, not a clan of undead athletes!"

"Look, I'm sorry. I tried, and I thought you were gonna listen. And then Stacy came along and—"

"I know," I said. Honestly, I couldn't blame Clayton. I'd gotten into this mess all by myself.

"If it matters, I did try to follow you. But I actually ended up with detention."

I blinked at him. "You?"

"Ladybell found me in the girls' locker room." He shrugged, his face coloring pink.

I couldn't help but smile at that. I mean, the idea that he'd actually followed me into the girls' locker room made me feel all warm and fuzzy. "Thanks for trying," I said, looking at my shoes.

"You're welcome."

"All right," Jenny said. "We've established Clayton's not a complete jerk. Can we now hear what he knows?"

"Right. Sure," Clayton said. "You *are* a vampire." That he directed straight toward me, his eyes warm and apologetic. "Sorry. No two ways around that. But you're not necessarily *stuck* as a vampire. But if you feed off a live person, then you will be stuck."

"And again I ask—you know this how?"

He made a face, and I could tell he didn't want to reveal his source, but I also knew he could tell I was serious. "My grandpa," he finally said.

"Your grandpa?" Jenny repeated.

"Yeah. He knows a lot about this stuff. He's the one who gave me the stake."

"So by *knows a lot* you mean he hunts vampires?" I was so not liking this man. I mean, unless he wanted to hunt Stephen Wills. And then I'd adopt him as my own grandpa.

"Yeah," Clayton said. "I think he's gonna want to meet you."

"No way," I said, shaking my head. "No way, no way, no way! I'm not getting staked by you *or* your grandpa!"

"He won't stake you. Not after I tell him you're okay."

"And you'd tell him that?"

He looked at me for a second, then one shoulder lifted and dropped. "Yeah. Sure. I mean, I really do think you're okay."

And then, he smiled.

Wow. I mean, I know he was talking about okay in the vampire sense, but there was just something about his eyes.

I mean, why hadn't I ever noticed before how cute Clayton Greene was?

And then Jenny (who I honestly don't think realized what was going on) popped the top on a Diet Coke she'd gotten from the fridge and said, "Well, she's not going to see Gramps until you talk with him first, that's for sure. You're not taking my best friend to someone who might decide to kill her! I mean, who'd help me with trig if Beth wasn't around?"

"I could help you," Clayton said.

"Oh," Jenny said. "Right. Well, okay then."

"Guys!" I screamed, and they both laughed. I did, too. And for the first time in a long time I felt normal. I even felt alive.

It was nice. And it reminded me just how much I wanted to get un-undead.

I sat up straighter, shaking off the warm fuzzies. Time to get down to business. "Okay, so Clayton's gonna tell his grandpa about me—"

"And when I'm certain he won't drive a stake through your heart," Clayton finished as I winced, "I'll introduce you to him. He can fill you in on the whole not-being-a-vamp-anymore thing."

"What can I do?" Jenny asked.

I looked her dead in the eye. "Help me think of a way to get back at Stephen Wills. I want revenge," I said. "Against all of them."

CHAPTER 16

To Jenny's credit—and to Clayton's—they were both totally with me on the Get Even plan.

"What about Tamara and Stacy and the other cheerheads?" Jenny asked. "Are they vamps, too?"

I shook my head. "No way. I see Stacy in first period all the time. And all those cheerleader car washes earlier this year?" Tamara and Stacy both love nothing better than to put on a tiny bikini, stand on a corner, and lure college boys to a parking lot to get their car washed. Clearly the sun wasn't among their personal problems.

"They're Renfields," Clayton said, and both Jenny and I stared at him blankly. He sighed, exasperated, then explained. "Helpers," he said. "They help the vamps. Like Renfield in the Bram Stoker novel."

"Wasn't Renfield completely whacked?" I asked.

"And you think Tamara's not?"

We all got a nice chuckle out of that. But whether Tamara was nuts or not, I got the point. She wasn't a vamp;

she was an assistant. I figured Stacy was as well. And the rest of the cheer-heads, too. (Although why they'd want to date vampires is beyond me! I mean, Chris is obnoxious on the best of days, and Ennis is ten times as bad. What Stacy and Melissa saw in them . . . I just didn't get it!)

"The sun thing," Jenny said, looking as if her thoughts were a million miles away. "That explains the gloves and greasepaint."

Now it was Clayton's turn to stare, completely clueless.

"Don't you remember? We even did an article in the paper. About how our football team was setting a fashion trend because some of the players wore gloves and had that black goop all over the faces and not just under their eyes. And Stephen was at the top of the list."

"Makes sense," Clayton said. "Before the time change, they'd have to deal with day games."

"And the uniform and black goop kept the sun away," I said.

Jenny rolled her eyes. "And they were acting like they did it because they were cool."

"I need you to corner the girls," I said to Jenny. "They must know the jocks are vamps. Figure out what else they know. And figure out why the girls aren't fanged out."

"Me?" Jenny squeaked.

"Well, duh. I can hardly do it. I'll turn into a crispy critter if I try to go to school. Because I'm not wearing greasepaint or a football uniform. That's for sure!"

"Oh." She frowned. "Right." The frown got even deeper. "But, Beth, you've *got* to go to school. Your parents will kill you if your GPA drops, and you know you'll get dinged if you miss days!"

She had a point. Not only would my parents kill me (again?), but my chances of getting into Tisch (assuming they accept the undead or assuming I'm fixable) would nose-dive. Not to mention that Clayton would slide into the valedictorian slot, and that was something I simply could *not* let happen. Even if he was cute.

Trouble was, I didn't really see an alternative. "How can I go to school? School is during the day!"

"Yeah, but it's inside. You should be fine during the day so long as you're inside."

"Should be? This is my life—well, *death*—that we're talking about. I don't want to be a human French fry!"

"You were in the dirt, right?" Jenny said. "That's like being inside. And when your finger went outside, it got burned. *Only* it. You said so yourself."

I nodded. "True." Now we were getting somewhere. If I were inside, I'd be okay. "Actually," I said to Clayton, "Chris and Ennis were both in the caf on Monday. And they were on the field last night. And they both wear the gloves and greasepaint during games."

"So they're probably vamps, too!" Jenny finished. "I bet that's why Elise broke up with Chris!"

I squinted at her. "You think she knows he's a vampire?"

She considered the question. "Okay. Probably not. It was only a theory."

I tapped my foot. "Can we focus our theories on relevant subjects and avoid things like, oh, other people's love lives?"

"I was *trying* to be relevant," Jenny said indignantly. "The fact that Chris and Ennis were in the caf must mean that you're okay walking around inside the school, too. I mean, so long as you avoid windows."

"Did you read the *Waterloo Watch*?" Clayton asked. "The Watcher said they've got some kind of neurological disorder." He snorted. "Yeah, Ennis is so not right in the head." He chuckled.

"You read the *Watch*?" Jenny asked.

"Sure. It's a hoot."

She and I exchanged satisfied glances. "But I think Jenny's got a point."

"If Chris and Ennis are vamps then you can definitely go to school during the day, too."

"At least after lunch," Jenny said. "Maybe that's why they miss all their morning classes. They're hanging upside down with their bat buddies or something."

"Jenny . . ." I said, a warning note in my voice. I really didn't want to think about sleeping upside down in some cave. Yuck!

"Sorry," she said.

"At any rate," Clayton said, "I think we're right. So long as you're not in direct sunlight, you're okay."

"Yeah, but what am I supposed to do?" I asked. "Go to school every morning before the sun's up? The school isn't even unlocked then!"

Clayton got up and opened the fridge, then stared at the contents.

"Um, hello?" Normally, that wouldn't bother me, but considering my only source of food was in plastic pouches in my bathroom, I wasn't feeling the warm glow of hospitality.

"Sorry," he said. "Can I snag a soda?"

"You got a solution to my problem?"

He hooked his thumbs in his belt loops and leaned against the freezer side of the fridge. All in all a very James Dean–ish sort of look. "Yup."

"Oh." That was surprising. Good, but surprising. "Well, what?"

"Ms. Shelby," he said, referring to the journalism teacher. "Tell her you want to come in early and work on the layout for the Christmas wrap-up issue." We do a big issue right before Christmas break, sort of summarizing all the stuff that's happened so far in the year. I do spend a lot of time on it, so it really was a good excuse.

"But you'd have to be there before dawn," Jenny said. "No way is Ms. Shelby getting to school that early. I've got her for homeroom, and she's practically comatose in the morning."

"She'd give me a key," I said.

"She's not allowed to do that!" Jenny protested.

Jenny was right, but I was still pretty sure Ms. Shelby would do it anyway. I'm pretty much the teacher's pet. And the principal and a ton of other teachers love me, too. "She will," I said simply. "At least, I'm pretty sure she will."

"We'll tell her I'm working with you on it," Clayton said. "Between the two of us, she'll agree."

I looked at him, surprised—because who really wants to get to school *that* early—then nodded. "Yeah. That'll work."

"Okay," Jenny said. "What about me?"

I had the perfect answer to that. But with Clayton there, I couldn't say. I shot a quick look in his direction, then said, "I've got something in mind for you. Don't worry." I tried to telegraph that I expected the Watcher to help me out here, but as smart as Jenny can be at times, I don't think she got it.

Clayton looked at his watch. "I guess I should go," he said, then looked at me. "I'll meet you after dark tomorrow and we can plan more. I'll get the key from Ms. Shelby during class. So Thursday you can come back to school. In the meantime, just hang in your room. Tell your mom you're sick or something."

I made a face. "I almost forgot. I've been ordered to attend his majesty tomorrow after school."

"Stephen?" Jenny asked.

"Apparently the creep thinks I'm his little minion."

"Call me on your cell when you're done with Stephen," he said. "We'll meet up then and I'll give you the key."

I gaped. "First of all, I lost my cell phone. And second of all, you actually expect me to really meet with that creep?"

"Come on, Beth," he said. "Haven't you heard the saying? You keep your friends close, but your enemies closer."

Which is good advice, unless they happen to bite you. I learned *that* one the hard way.

CHAPTER 17

After Jenny and Clayton left Tuesday night, I spent a few hours pacing in my room, trying to figure out the best way to get back at Stephen and company. At about five-thirty in the morning, I remembered that I didn't keep curtains on my windows because I'd always loved waking up to the sun streaming in.

This morning, though, I was thinking that maybe wasn't such a great idea. Unless I wanted the worst sunburn of my life. Hahahaha. Um, no.

Fortunately, my mom was still at the office (I mean, it was after five a.m.! Why on earth should she be home with her kid?) so I didn't have to be quiet. I grabbed a roll of foil from the cabinet above the stove and a box of green Hefty garbage bags from under the sink. It took longer to find duct tape, but I finally found a roll in the laundry room. (I have no idea why it was there, but my mom can't sew. So maybe she figured she'd just tape any ripped seams back together?)

At any rate, I schlepped all of these tools back to my room, then realized that the favor my parents did by giving me a well-lit room was going to end up being *very* inconvenient.

There are six windows in my room, three facing east and three facing north. I had no idea what time the sun started coming up, but I figured it couldn't be too long now. So I spent a hectic few minutes trying to rip pieces of duct tape, tape foil onto the window, then cover the foil with a plastic bag. I wished I'd thought of this before Jenny and Clayton left, but I managed to get it done. In fact, I was just putting the last piece of tape in place when I started feeling incredibly sleepy. This room-darkening thing was exhausting!

I lay down on my bed and stared at my now-ugly walls. What they needed, I thought, was some color. Maybe if I went to Hancock Fabrics and bought some nice pink muslin, I could staple it up and over the . . .

CHAPTER 18

Okay. This passing-out-cold thing was getting a little old.

I woke up with a start, sitting bolt upright and trying not to scream. *Something* had startled me awake, and I was sure someone was in the house. I listened, though, and realized that I could hear just about everything going on around me. Including a little squeak that made me pretty sure that although we didn't have rats, we might have a family of mice living under the floorboards.

Rodents notwithstanding, I have to say that the preternatural-hearing thing was pretty cool. And it also convinced me that I was all alone.

My eyes drifted to my walls, and I realized I'd dozed off while I'd been planning to buy pink muslin. Although now that I thought about it, maybe red would be better. Bloodred, you know? Just for the irony.

I scooted to the edge of the bed and stretched, surprised I'd fallen asleep so quickly. I must have been more tired than I thought. My stomach rumbled, and I immediately thought of brownies. Right after that, I felt nauseous. So much for my future with chocolate.

I got up, intending to go through the kitchen to the garage. I'd put the blood from the sink back into the ice chest, then hidden the whole thing in the big freezer. Since my mom hasn't defrosted anything in months, I wasn't worried about being discovered.

I stopped in my doorway, though. Mom never shut the curtains, and it had been just a few minutes shy of sunrise when I'd finished covering my windows and had my little nap. That meant the house was UV Central, and I was stuck in this room until the sun went down.

I groaned, my stomach growling, as I turned to look at my clock. Exactly how many hours was I going to be stuck here, anyw—?

I stopped midthought. Because according to my clock, it was five-thirty-seven. I'd looked up sunset after Jenny left, so I'd be sure to meet Stephen at more or less the right time. And this was it. Sunset. Or, rather, a few minutes after.

I gaped at the clock, not quite believing. If that was true, then *I slept the entire freaking day!*

The sun had come up, and I'd crashed and burned (well, not literally, thank goodness). And now that I was awake, I had two big problems: one, getting to the bleachers before Stephen gave up and did some incredibly gory and mean master-minion thing to punish me. And two, actually going to school tomorrow if I couldn't manage to stay awake.

The first I solved by racing out the door and sprinting toward the school.

But the second . . . well, for that one, I didn't have a good solution at all.

CHAPTER 19

"You came," Stephen said as I stepped into the dark space under the bleachers. He stood in a shaft of moonlight, his skin glowing and his expression smug. I swear, if I'd had Clayton's stake right then, I would have taken care of him myself.

He held out a hand, my purse dangling from his finger-tips. I snatched it away from him, then opened it and pawed through the contents. Everything was there: wallet, pens, Stephen King paperback, cell phone. I checked the phone. The battery still had almost a full charge. I checked the wallet. Twenty-two dollars and my student ID. All in order.

I tucked everything back inside, then glanced at Stephen. But I didn't say thanks. I mean, it was his fault I'd lost the thing in the first place.

He chuckled softly, then smiled. "So very good to see you." Honestly, he looked like a guy who'd just convinced Miss America to suck face with him.

Since I wasn't sharing the love, I held back, my reacquired purse clutched to my chest.

He cocked his head, then held his hands out to his sides. "You're upset," he said. "Come on. It's okay. You can tell me."

I just stared. This . . . this . . . *creep* who'd turned me into something inhuman and undead was standing in front of me looking a lot like Heath Ledger in *Casanova*.

"Elizabeth," he cooed, then took my hand.

I ripped it back.

A second later, I wasn't so sure I should have done that. He snarled, wolflike, and bared fangs. "I don't mind that *you're* upset," he said. "But don't you dare invoke my wrath."

Invoke his wrath? What? Were we suddenly back in the dark ages?

I almost asked, but then I got a look at his face . . . and decided that invoking his wrath would definitely be a bad idea. I backed up a step, suddenly feeling a lot more compliant. "Right. Sorry. Um, yeah. I was a little ticked. But I'm better now. Now I'm just annoyed."

Wolf boy faded, replaced by Heath Ledger again, all kind and conciliatory. "Tell me it's not that bad," he said, circling me as he spoke. "I'd hate to think I've ruined your life."

"Golly no, Stephen. This is just peachy keen."

He laughed then and hooked an arm around my shoulder. Like I was his favorite little sister or something.

Monday, I would have been depressed that he thought of me all sisterly. Tonight, I really wished he weren't thinking of me at all.

"So, are you going to tell me why you did this to me? I

mean, you *did* do this to me, didn't you? You're a vampire, right?"

"You really are as smart as they say," he said.

"Chris Freytag, too," I said, just so he'd know I really wasn't an idiot. "And Ennis and Derek and Nelson."

He cocked his head just slightly, and I took that as a yes.

"How were Chris and Ennis at school?" I asked. "I mean, why aren't they asleep during the day? And what about the sun?"

Stephen just smiled. "If you can't figure out the answers to those questions on your own, Elizabeth, then maybe you're not as much use to me as I thought."

Oh.

Since that didn't sound good, I changed the subject. "So, is everybody on the team a vampire?"

"No," he said, then frowned a little. "Not yet."

"So what's the deal? You're running around making new vampires all the time? Working your way up to the whole team? The whole school?" *Whoa.* I just realized. Maybe he was working his way up to the whole town. A town full of vampires! Sort of like *Invasion of the Body Snatchers* or *'Salem's Lot.*

I was getting myself worked up, but Stephen was laughing. "The whole school?" He snorted. "I think not. We're very . . . selective. It's an honor, you know." He leaned in close, his face right next to mine. "You do realize it's an honor, don't you?"

I *wanted* to tell him he was a psycho-vampire and to not do me any more favors. Instead, I just said, "Well, yeah, sure. I mean, I ran all the way home and didn't even get winded. It's almost like being a superhero." And you know what? A tiny little part of me meant that.

I stifled a shiver. This was *not* a good thing. I did not

want to be a vampire. I did not like being a vampire. Night vision and Nike speed notwithstanding.

Still, at least I sounded sincere. If Stephen's bs meter was turned on, it wouldn't give me away.

Or would it? I wondered about that a second later as Stephen leaned in close to me, then sniffed, his nostrils flaring with the action.

I took a step back. "Um, hello?"

"You have drunk," he said, "but you haven't yet fed."

He could tell all that by sniffing me? "Is that bad?" I asked, hoping I sounded innocent.

"Hmmm," he said.

"So, you said you weren't changing the whole town into vamps," I said briskly, trying to change the subject. "But you never answered me about the football team."

He leaned back, resting against the underside of the bleachers, all casual in his tight jeans and crisp white T-shirt. Honestly, if I didn't already know he was an undead creep, I'd think he looked pretty adorable.

"Not yet," he said, finally answering my question. "Someday, maybe, but not until . . ." He trailed off, then pushed away from the bleachers and hooked his arm through mine. I managed to stifle a shiver and congratulated myself on my nerves of steel. "Actually, you're the last we're admitting to our little honors program, Elizabeth. At least for a while. We handpicked you. No," he amended. "*I* handpicked you."

"Yeah," I said. "So you told me. Why?"

He smiled, full of southern charm. "You really are a cut-to-the-chase kind of girl, aren't you?"

I shrugged. "Maybe."

"Fair enough. It's simple, really. I gave you a gift. A superhero's life. You said so yourself, right?"

I nodded slowly, warily.

"So now it's your turn to do something for me."

"Oh." I frowned. What could I possibly do for him? Because if he was thinking sex, he'd pretty much lost his chance once he spiked my drink and bit my neck. "Um, what is it you want me to do?"

Again with the smile. "Nothing you won't enjoy."

"I don't know, Stephen. I mean—"

"Elizabeth," he said sharply. "I thought I explained the rules. I say 'jump,' and you say 'how high?'" He chucked my chin. "And don't go getting any ideas about killing me."

"Um, why would I want to do that?" I asked, innocently.

"It's a gift I've given you," he said. "But sometimes people don't appreciate the things they've been handed." As he spoke, he handed me a wooden stake. "Try," he said.

I held it, dumbstruck, even as my mind screamed for me to *do it! Do it! Do it!*

"Try," he repeated again, this time with an edge to his voice.

I lashed out with all my pent-up fury, aiming the point at his heart. It connected and I felt an instant of triumph before the pain set in. The stake had burst into flames, singeing my hand along with it.

I screamed, dropping what was left of the burning wood and clutching my wounded hand.

"You should cover that," Stephen said, handing me a glove.

I cringed, still cradling my hand. He shook the glove, impatient, until I took it. I slid it on, glaring at him the whole time.

"I told you, Elizabeth. I'm your master. And a minion cannot kill her master. For that matter, you can't kill any member above you in the clan. Or equal to you in the hierarchy, for that matter."

"Equal to me?"

"With the same master," he said.

"Oh." I cocked my head. "So who is Chris's master?"

A flash of anger colored his eyes, and I winced. "Watch yourself, Elizabeth. You'll do that for me, won't you?"

I waited a beat, which pretty much exhausted my courage. Then I nodded. "Sure." What else could I say? I wasn't going to risk pissing Stephen off. I mean, my hand got burned because of his little demonstration. Who knew what the consequences would be if he actually set out to punish me. Maybe a slap on the wrist. Maybe a lot, lot worse.

Until I knew what exactly I was up against, I was Cooperation Girl. "So, can I ask you a question?"

"You can ask anything."

"Right. Um. Were you . . . I mean, when you transferred to Waterloo . . . were you already a vamp?"

He laughed. "Oh, yes. I've been a vampire for quite a long time."

"How long?" I asked, suspicious.

"Two hundred and thirty-three years," he said, as if he was talking about the weather.

"Oh." Well, that explains the formal way of talking. Old habits die hard, I guess. "So why does a two-hundred-and-thirty-three-year-old vampire want to come to a Texas high school?"

"To play football, of course."

Why did that *not* surprise me?

"Ah, Elizabeth. I'm so glad you're taking an interest. You really are an exceptional girl."

I managed a simpering smile and decided to drop the questions for now. "Right. So, um, what do you want me to do?" Now I was Cooperation Girl *and* Helper Girl. Oh, joy.

He looked at me, his eyes narrow, as if he was trying to

figure out if I was sincere. Then he cocked his head and smiled.

I didn't like the look of that smile at all.

"Come with me," he said, holding out his hand.

I hesitated. "Where are we going?"

"You're a creature of the night now, Elizabeth. We're going to see some of the nightlife."

"Oh."

I must have looked nervous, because he laughed. "We're going to Sixth Street, my dear," he said, referring to Austin's well-known after-hours hangout, lined with restaurants, bars, and clubs with live music.

"Oh. Well, okay, then." Even though most of the clubs card, some let in underage kids, stamping our hands so that we're not served the dreaded alcohol.

"And while we're there," Stephen added casually, "we'll get you a little snack." I looked up sharply, but he smiled, as innocent as an angel. "Trust me, Elizabeth. You think you have superpowers now . . . but once you've tasted the wine of the vein . . . well, then you'll see the true nature of your new powers."

CHAPTER 20

Austin is home to the University of Texas, and Sixth Street is where a lot of the UT students can be found. Apparently even on a Wednesday night.

And, I learned from Stephen, Sixth Street is where a lot of the local vampires hang out. (Interestingly, those bats I mentioned live only six blocks down at the bridge over the river. Talk about the right atmosphere for an undead convention.)

I wasn't really interested in the local undead crowd, though. I was interested in Stephen. And Chris. And the other Waterloo High vamps. I mean, I'd love to say that I was all motivated to save my hometown from the evil scourge that is *vampyre*, but the truth was I was really only interested in saving me. Selfish? Maybe. But at least I'm honest.

Anyway, it didn't much matter, because Stephen was in charge. We were in his BMW and we cruised through downtown, finally parking in front of a club on Sixth Street near the freeway. What used to be the seedier end, but now was considered cool, even with the tattoo parlors and walk-in body piercing storefronts.

"We're here," he said, his smile giving me chills. And not the good kind.

"Here," it turned out, was a little club called the Night Light. The guy at the door looked at Stephen, nodded, and ushered us into a whole other world. Loud music. Lots of student-age kids drinking and playing pool and throwing darts. Lots of laughing and dancing.

Honestly, the place looked like *fun*.

And that's when I noticed something really weird. Clusters of popular kids in the corners. Student council. Band leaders. More jocks. And a few kids I didn't recognize, but who I guessed were college students.

Okay, that wasn't all that weird. I mean, it's no secret that almost every senior has a fake ID. But here's the weird part: there, among the cool kids and the college students, I saw Richie Carter. And Tony Bart, a total math geek. And Deborah O'Keefe, who barely beat me out last year in a chess club tournament. And a whole slew of kids who normally choose staying at home playing video games or finishing their homework over hanging with the popular crowd.

But here they were, all standing around, looking like they were having a blast. Playing darts, drinking (Cokes, I presume), and mingling (with each other, not with the popular kids). And, I noticed, each and every one of them had a Band-Aid on their neck.

Whoa, Nellie.

I was, of course, immediately suspicious. "Why are they here? For that matter, why are we here?"

"I told you," Stephen said. "Dinner."

And that's when I saw Tamara and Stacy. They were playing pool with a couple of college-aged boys, and flirting like you wouldn't believe. Stacy was tossing around her oh-so-fabulous hair, and Tamara was leaning waaaaay over the pool table until she was about to fall out of her top. Melissa was there, too, laughing and flirting, which was *really* odd since she and Ennis have been attached at the hip for so many years.

I looked around, but I didn't see Ennis or the other jocks anywhere. Just as well. If Ennis saw Melissa flirting, he'd surely beat the flirtee to a bloody pulp.

I turned to Stephen, my mouth gaping open since I couldn't quite form the question.

He nodded and laughed and told me to make myself at home. And to let him know if I saw anyone who looked appetizing.

Oh. My. God.

I sort of scooted over to a corner, wondering how I was going to get out of this. The whole ick factor aside, drinking from someone's neck would mean that I'd stay a vampire. And at the moment, I really didn't like the company that meant I'd have to keep!

So I stood there in my little corner. Just watching until Stephen came over, Derek wandering behind him.

"Hello, little girl," Derek said, then leered at me. "Too bad you're one of us now. I would've liked to take a bite out of you."

"Leave her alone," Stephen said, his voice sharper than I would have expected.

Derek backed off, an air of false conciliation on his face. "Yes, sir. Can't be messing with the brilliant Beth Frasier, the girl who's going to pave the way to recruiting guys and girls. She's too import—"

"Shut up," Stephen hissed, and Derek's pale face went even paler. "Now go," Stephen said, shoving at Derek's shoulder. "Go and feed. That's all you're good for anyway. Lately you haven't even been playing a decent game. Careful, or Coach will cut you."

I thought I saw fear flash in Derek's eyes, but it was gone in a second. So was he, for that matter, disappearing toward a dark corner of the bar.

I stayed still, wishing I could melt away. Since I couldn't, it was almost a relief when Stephen asked me to dance. At least on a dance floor I could think about the music and not the commotion in my head.

Dancing with Stephen was . . . hypnotic. I'm not sure if I have a different feeling of time now, but hours flew by, until I finally begged to stop. (I couldn't even say I was tired! I wasn't at all!)

I was back to leaning against the wall, scowling and wishing I could go home, when a lanky blond boy—probably about nineteen—came over. "Hey there," he said. "I'm thinking you're too young to be in here."

I made a face. "I don't recall asking you," I said. "And the fact is, I don't want to be here."

He grinned. I guess it didn't bother him that I was being so rude. "Me neither," he said. "My brother dragged me along. This isn't my scene."

"Yeah?" I was starting to like this guy.

He motioned toward the bar. "I'm Kevin, by the way. Do you want something to eat? To drink?"

I shook my head, suddenly aware of the rumbling in my stomach and the tingling in my teeth. Oh, man. All the dancing with Stephen had the effect of working up my appetite. And suddenly all I could think about was being in a dark alley with this guy . . . and *not* because he was cute!

I turned away sharply, afraid he'd see something scary in my eyes, and ended up looking toward an empty darkish corner. Or I thought it was empty. Then I saw there was a staircase in the back. And I saw Ennis standing there, his eyes kind of glazed over, as if he'd just gorged on Thanksgiving dinner.

He was looking across the room, and I turned, following the direction of his stare. Tamara was looking back at him, even though this totally gorgeous college guy was leaning over her, showing her how to hold a cue stick.

I saw her smile up at the guy in her flirtiest smile, blow him a sexy kiss, and then I saw her glance at Ennis.

And then I saw her nod.

Whoa. Tamara and Ennis? What was going on here?

"That's my brother," Kevin said. I'd totally forgotten about him. I looked where he was looking and realized he was talking about Tamara's little boy toy. I frowned even more, now *really* wondering what was going on.

But I didn't need the details to know that this was some serious ammunition.

I glanced sharply down at my purse. "Did you hear that? I think my phone just rang."

Kevin didn't argue, though he must think I have supernatural hearing since it was impossible to hear anything over the blare of the speakers. I pulled my phone out and pretended to answer, but really, I was turning on the camera. And then I was aiming the little lens toward Tamara, and then . . .

Click!

A lovely little candid shot for the *Watch*. Oh yeah. Her platform for the Voice of Waterloo contest might be virtue and self-esteem, but Little Miss Virtue was going down.

I said good-bye to my pretend caller, then half smiled at Kevin, who was watching me curiously. I wasn't worried, though. Even if he knew what I was doing, he had no reason to rat me out. I mean, why would a college boy care about Tamara?

"I'm going to go get some water," I said, then I stepped away before he could answer. I had my phone back out, this time set to voice record. I held it up to my ear, pretending to talk, but really I had my finger on the record button, and I was moving through the crowd, trying to pick up snippets. About the time I got to the pool table, Tamara had stepped away from her boy toy and moved over to Stephen. *This,* I thought, *ought to be good.*

Except when I got near they shut up.

Fine. I've watched enough spy movies to know what to do. I hit the button to keep recording, surreptitiously dropped my phone casually into a seat cushion, aimed a simpering smile at Stephen, then moved on toward the bar.

College Kevin met me there. "So how come you're here? You said this isn't your regular hangout?"

"Um, no."

"Well, I'm glad to see you, anyway." He leaned close and brushed my hand with his. His, I noticed, was wet. And not with water, either. Because whatever was on his hand made me start itching.

Since I didn't want to look like a baboon scratching myself while talking to a cute guy, though, I ignored it. And, since I'm totally incompetent at talking with cute guys, I looked at the floor and muttered something completely unintelligible.

Clearly, I am a dating nightmare.

Kevin must have picked up on my nervousness, because he didn't say anything more. He just stood there next to me in a comfortable (for him, anyway) silence. I finally got the nerve to lift my head, and I noticed that Ennis was on his way back up the stairs. Derek was coming down, a glassy look in his eyes. He shot me a quick grin as he passed, and I recoiled, seeing that his fangs were bared and the tips stained red. I swallowed, hoping Kevin hadn't noticed.

He hadn't. Okay, good. One bullet dodged.

I wasn't sure what to do about the next bullet, though. Because Tamara had left Stephen and gone back to Kevin's brother by the pool table. Now she'd taken his hand and was leading him up the stairs.

And all of a sudden, I understood what was going on. When Stephen had said dinner was served, he'd meant it literally. This was our own little vampire buffet, with Tamara and Stacy leading the cows to slaughter.

And many of the cows looked remarkably like my fellow students.

I looked around, feeling a little frantic, and saw Stephen watching me. I tried to look all casual and cool—like I hung out in vampire dining clubs all the time—but I'm not sure he bought it.

When he came over, he flashed a quick smile, then looked Kevin up and down. "There's more to do upstairs," he said. "You two should check it out."

He spoke casually, but I heard the command, and considering that I was still stuck playing Cooperation Girl, I smiled and told him thanks. Then I smiled even broader at Kevin. "I've heard they have air hockey up there," I said. "One game?"

Stephen was moving away from us, but I saw him nod in approval. Kevin nodded, too. So I guess the gig was on. I just wasn't sure what to do.

I knew I had to do something, but my mind was sadly blank. And when Kevin took my hand, it went even blanker. Not only am I not used to holding hands with college boys, but suddenly I was Hungry. With a capital H. A big, bold, bloody capital H.

I needed to get out of there.

More, I needed to somehow save Kevin (from me) and Kevin's brother (from whoever was waiting up the stairs). And if I could save a few other kids, well, more power to me.

I didn't know what to do, though. More important, I didn't know what to do without getting caught. So much for being the smartest girl in school. I was seeing my GPA in a whole new—utterly useless—way.

At any rate, I knew I had to play the game, so I followed Kevin to the stairs, scooping up my phone and dropping it in my pocket. The stairs were dark, and Kevin was moving slowly. I could see just fine, but had to pretend to plod along, too. I was desperately trying to decide how to get out of this, when all hell broke loose.

The overhead sprinklers spurted to life, and at the same time an ear-splitting wail cut through the din of the party-goers. Kevin grabbed my hand. "Fire!"

Above us, on the landing, I saw his brother rush out, looking not the least bit glazed over. I expected Ennis to follow, but he never showed. And Kevin's brother looked to be in fine condition. So maybe I was wrong? Maybe Tamara hadn't led him up to the slaughter?

But where was Ennis? Apparently Melissa was wondering the same thing, because she stood by the pool table and screamed for him until someone finally grabbed her arm and jerked her toward the exit.

"Kevin!" the brother shouted over the din. "Get out of here!"

Kevin turned to me, grabbing my shoulders. "You come, too," he said. "It's not safe here."

"Safe?" I repeated, stupidly.

"The place is on fire!" he shouted, his voice rising over the wail of the alarm.

I tried to answer, but his brother had clambered down the stairs and was pulling Kevin away. Kevin shot me one last glance, then followed his brother, tossing back a cry of "Run!" as he bolted through the back doors.

I started to follow that advice, then found myself tossed up against the wall, Stephen's hands clasped to my shoulders. "You little fool!"

I struggled to get free, but it wasn't any use. "What are you talking about?"

"Who were you talking to?" he demanded. "Tell me who that was!"

I tried to control my breathing, tried to stay calm. Something was going on here that I didn't understand, and I needed to play it very, very cool. "I don't know his name," I lied.

"Don't lie to me, Elizabeth. You stood here talking with him for fifteen minutes."

"I did what *you* told me to do!" I spat back. "And you practically insisted that he was my dinner."

He shook me. "And?"

"And I didn't want to know his name! I mean, if I'd known the cow was named Bessie, I never would have eaten hamburgers."

He stared at me, and I stared back, trying very, very hard not to freak out. And then something softened in his expression, and he let me go. I rubbed my shoulders, sure I had ten bruises, one for each finger.

"What's going on?" I demanded. The question was legitimate, but the bravado in my voice was a total act.

"Go home," he said.

I blinked at him. "You want me to go home?" I could hardly believe my luck. "What about you? The fire?"

"The fire was a ruse." He was looking in the direction that Kevin had gone, not at me, and I allowed myself a very quiet sigh of relief.

"Oh. But—"

"Go. We can't have your parents suspicious. You need to act like everything is exactly the same."

"Oh, sure," I said. "Except for the fact that I sleep all day and drink blood and the sun turns me into a crispy critter!" Not, I thought, that my parents would notice.

"With regard to your sleep habits, you will require less the older you get. In the meantime, I highly recommend caffeine." Great. I need legitimate vampire survival tips and he gives me sarcasm!

"As for the sun," he continued, "for that I might have a more practical suggestion." He reached into the back pocket of his jeans and drew out a piece of paper. He held it out to me and I took it, but I didn't unfold it. Not right away.

Stephen didn't press me to, either, but after a few minutes, I couldn't stand it anymore. I opened the paper and found myself looking at . . . Latin.

Huh? "What's this?"

"You're the smart one," Stephen said. "If you can find the answer, you'll be our salvation." He shrugged then, all casual and cool, but with a dangerous glint in his eye. "And if you *can't* find the answer . . . well, then I'm not sure if we really have any use for you after all."

CHAPTER 21

Right before the sun came up I tried what Stephen said. Caffeine, I mean. My mom had come and gone at some point (apparently without worrying about me) and there was still coffee in the pot. I poured a cup, noticing when I did that my formerly burned hand was all healed.

The coffee was cold, so I stuck it in the microwave until it was a reasonable temperature. I sniffed it tentatively, remembering my reaction to the milk I'd drunk. But Stephen had said it would keep me awake during the day, and even if he was a total jerk, I had to admit that he probably knew about stuff like that.

So I drank.

And then I retched. Down on my hands and knees I went, my stomach cramping as I vomited up the tiny bit of coffee I'd drunk and an entire bag's worth of blood.

Honestly, if my mom saw that mess, she'd kill me!

And if I saw Stephen Wills, I was going to kill him. In

fact, I thought, that was about the only punishment worthy of my revenge plan.

Even though I couldn't stake the jerkwad, somehow I was going to kill Stephen Wills.

I didn't have time to think about my plan any further, though, because the sun was coming up. I was safe in my darkened bedroom, of course, but thinking was impossible. My mind was too fuzzy, and the world was turning black.

CHAPTER 22

I woke up, saw two pairs of eyes peering down at me, and sat up screaming. About half a second later, I realized that the eyes belonged to Jenny and Clayton.

"Time?" I muttered, still groggy.

"Just after sunset," Clayton said. "We waited around for your mom to let us in, but we never saw her."

"I used the key you hide under the tomato plant pot," Jenny explained.

I didn't care how they got in, I was just glad to see them. "Did you bring my homework? I'm going to be soooo far behind!"

They exchanged glances, and I decided not to press the point. Maybe they were right; maybe I had better things to worry about than falling behind in homework.

"Okay, never mind. But what happened at school?" I looked at Jenny since I'd e-mailed her the picture of Tamara from my phone. So far, I hadn't had time to listen to the recording. But the picture was golden. "Any interesting gossip? Wild rumors? Anything?"

"A little of both," Clayton said. "Ennis wasn't around today."

"Not that that's any great loss," Jenny said. "Except that Tamara and Stacy were acting all weird. And I saw Melissa in the bathroom by the band hall, and she looked like she'd been crying. Did something happen with him?"

"I don't know." I told them about the club. About how so many of the less-than-popular crowd had been there, and about how I'd seen Kevin's brother come out, but not Ennis. "But what could have—"

"He staked him," Clayton said. "Ennis is dust."

I got a really queer feeling in the pit of my stomach. "*Staked* him! As in, he's dead?"

"I'd bet my autographed Stan Lee number one *Spider-man* comic," Clayton said.

"But—"

"My grandpa's heard rumors," Clayton said. "About some college guys coming in and hunting the local vampires. I think you may have met one of them."

"Oh, God," I said. "Do you think he—"

"Knows you're one, too?"

I nodded, suddenly unable to form words.

"I doubt it," Clayton said. "I mean, he told you to run, right? I bet he thinks you were just innocently there. You'd said it wasn't your scene, right? And it wasn't as if you were feeding . . ." He squinted. "Were you?"

I smacked him in the chest. "Of course not!"

"Well, then. I think you're cool."

"And maybe it'll end up working out great," Jenny said. "I mean, if they're on to Stephen and kill him . . . well, then you're no longer Stephen's minion, right? I mean, this

Kevin guy and his brother could be doing you a huge favor."

"Maybe," I said. But something about the whole Vampire Killers As My New Best Friends plan didn't sound right to me. "I'm not sure . . ."

"Doesn't matter right now anyway," Clayton said. "They don't go to Waterloo. They're not our immediate problem."

I perked up at that. The way he said "our," I mean. "Our problem." Yeah. That sounded nice.

"The Watcher heard about the bar, too," Jenny said, which was a terrible conversational segue, but I forgave her since I was dying to know what she'd done with the pic.

"Yeah? Tell!"

Jenny's eyes lit up. "Well, apparently the Watcher got ahold of some picture of Tamara at the club, leaning all over some college guy. And the Watcher posted it with a scathing commentary about how her little campaign to be the Voice of Waterloo didn't seem to be meshing with reality. *Everyone* was talking about it today. And Tamara spent most of the day surrounded by cheerleaders and so totally *not* holding court."

"It really was pretty awesome," Clayton said. "Definitely took her down a peg or two."

"The Watcher suggested that the students should look to someone a little more representative of the school at large."

"Like you or me," Clayton said, rolling his eyes. "Which was about the only stupid thing the Watcher said in the post."

I fought a laugh and tried very hard not to look at Jenny. Considering my newfound creature of the night status, I didn't think I could swing the television appearances. But I still appreciated her loyalty.

"But the biggest news is that we got the key to the school," Clayton said, holding it up for emphasis. "Shelby didn't even blink. She thinks we're golden, you know."

I almost corrected him on the "we" but decided not to. Honestly, it was true. And I really didn't want to risk pissing Clayton off. Academic arch-nemesis or not, he was still the only person I knew who had any practical advice for my current quandary.

"So we go tomorrow," he added.

I nodded, swinging my legs to the side of the bed and realizing I'd fallen asleep (passed out, really) in my clothes. I decided that was good. Clayton didn't need to see me in my Hello Kitty jammies.

As soon as my feet hit the floor, though, I remembered. "I still don't know how I can go to school. I pass out at the first hint of light. I mean, teacher's pet or not, even I can't get away with sleepwalking through class!"

"Stephen wouldn't tell you how Chris was at school during lunch?" Jenny asked. She didn't mention Ennis, but I saw the crease on her forehead. I understood it, too. Was I in line to get staked?

I shook my head, trying to focus. "He says if I can't figure it out myself then I'm obviously not smart enough and he made a mistake making me in the first place." I gritted my teeth. "He sure as heck *did* make a mistake!"

Clayton squinted at me. "He made you because you're smart?"

"Yeah," I said. "I'll tell you all about it, but I have to figure out this school day thing first. All he'd tell me to do was rely on caffeine. But I tried this morning. I drank a cup of coffee and ended up puking my guts out." I shivered with the memory. That had been *so* not fun!

"But if you can't drink coffee . . ." Jenny said.

"Yeah, I know. I need to figure this out."

"Come on," Clayton said, heading for my door. "If anyone knows the answer, it'll be my grandpa."

"The one who hunts vampires?" I asked.

"That's the one," Clayton said. He grinned. "But don't worry. I told him you were one of the good ones. At least, for now you are."

I wasn't entirely sure that made me feel better. But I stood up anyway. I mean, what choice did I have? I needed help. And if I couldn't have my own mom or dad or grandma or grandpa, then, well, I guess I'd take what I could get. And hope to heck the old man didn't decide to stake me.

Considering *that* charming thought, I dragged my feet a little as we all schlepped to Clayton's beat-up Buick Skylark, complete with a coat of primer, a Keep Austin Weird bumper sticker, and upholstery with more stuffing on the outside than the in. I didn't complain, though. I had no mode of transportation and no heartbeat, so I wasn't in the mood to dis other people's belongings.

As Clayton drove, I told him and Jenny about the piece of paper Stephen had given me.

"Latin?" Clayton said.

"A photocopy," I clarified. "But it looks like the original was really old." I started to pull it out of my pocket, but he waved a hand. "Wait until we get to my grandpa's. I can't look while I'm driving, anyway."

I almost offered it to Jenny, but considering she still had trouble with second conjugation verbs, I doubted she'd be able to translate it anyway. Besides, she didn't seem too interested. Instead, when I swiveled in my seat to look at her behind me, I saw that she looked a little sick.

"Jenny?"

She shook her head. "It's just so freaky. Vampires and

weird Latin texts. And all those kids at the club with Band-Aids on their necks. And I bet not one of them will remember how they got it."

"I know," I said. I thought about my conversation with Elise. A bug bite, she'd said, and I really didn't get the feeling she was lying. But why didn't she remember?

The whole situation gave me the shivers, and I wished that it was all over. Done. And Stephen The Jerk Wills was a big, hairy pile of dust.

The thing was, I wanted revenge for me. But I also wanted it for all the students that Stephen and his crew had fed off of. All the geeks and so-called losers that these popular kids thought were lower on the food chain. They weren't. And somehow, I was going to prove that.

I just didn't know how.

CHAPTER 23

Clayton's grandpa lived in a trailer park just off Barton Springs Road. One of those weird Austin things that you can't quite figure out how it's managed to exist even though Austin is more Silicon Valley than hippy-dippy these days. But there it was. A bunch of trailers on a large lot stuck between two popular restaurants. One of the "most coveted pieces of property in Austin," as my mom would say.

Me, I thought it was kind of cool. I mean, it had character, anyway. Just like Leslie, the guy who stands on corners downtown wearing a gold lamé bikini in the middle of winter. I think he ran for mayor once. Or city council or something. I don't think he won, but he could have. Austin's a weird town, after all.

Anyway, the trailer park had lots of pecan trees, and the full moon cast shadows through the leaves. Clayton moved slowly toward the back, finally parking in front of a small-ish trailer with a little wooden porch attached. An American flag flew from a pole stuck through the porch, and a

Protected by Smith & Wesson bumper sticker was plastered on the door.

The door, I also noticed, was rimmed with garlic. I eyed it suspiciously, wondering if I was going to melt into a pool of goo if I touched it or pass out if I smelled it. Clayton saw me looking. "Don't worry," he said, "it'll only affect you after your first kill."

"Oh," I said. "Right."

Beside me, Jenny made a little sound. Honestly, I think this whole thing was getting to be too much for her.

Clayton knocked, and a few seconds later, the door opened a crack, revealing a grizzled old man in a plaid shirt and blue jeans. He ignored Clayton, but stared directly at me. "So you're the vampire," he said, his voice raspy from what had to have been a ton of cigarettes.

"Yeah," I said. "I guess I am."

"Grandpa," Clayton said, "this is Beth Frasier. Beth, my grandpa, Arvin Greene."

He looked me up and down, then finally turned to Clayton. "You're sure she hasn't fed?"

"I trust her," he said. And then he reached over and took my hand. I felt that odd little tingle again, only this time it wasn't in my teeth; it was all over my body. And it felt really nice.

"Hmmph," the old man said. Then he stepped out onto the patio and stood right in front of me. "You turn out to be some evil bloodsucker who's dragged my grandson into this and I'll drive a stake through your heart faster than you can say Count Dracula."

I blanched a little, but nodded, even as Clayton said, "Grandpa! Shut up, already!"

But Grandpa wasn't listening. Instead, he held up a spray bottle and squirted me straight in the face!

"Ah!" I yelped. And whatever he sprayed me with itched like crazy. I scratched like mad with the pads of my fingers (because every girl knows that breaking the skin on your face can leave scars). "What *is* that stuff?"

"Holy water," he said. Then he snorted. "And you didn't burn."

"I *told* you," Clayton said.

"Told him what?" Jenny asked.

"That she hasn't fed yet."

"If she had," Grandpa said, "she'd have welts burned all over her face. As it is, she's just a little itchy."

"A lot itchy," I said. "Thanks a lot." But at least now I knew what Kevin had been up to. He really was hunting vampires. And he'd been testing me at the bar. Since I hadn't burned—and hadn't scratched—I'd passed.

Grandpa looked at me now, all smiles. "You're okay," he said. "For now." He headed back into the house, Clayton and Jenny following. I hung back, feeling a little stupid, then cleared my throat.

Grandpa turned around, smacked his forehead with his palm, and snorted. "Hmmph," he said with a chuckle. "Never have invited a vampire in before. Well, come on there, girl. You're welcome inside. At least until I find out you're evil."

Honestly, I didn't have a warm, fuzzy feeling about this!

We got settled, and after Gramps had passed out sodas to Jenny and Clayton (both of whom shot me apologetic looks), I recited yet again everything that had happened to me. I ended by mentioning the weird Latin document and our problem with me going to school.

Grandpa snorted. "Thought you said you were smart, girlie."

I glared. I was getting a little bit tired of that comeback.

But before I could think of something to say, he got up and went to a cabinet over the sink in his tiny kitchen.

I'm not sure what I was expecting, but when he returned with a box of Vivarin, I knew it wasn't that. "Caffeine," he said. "Just like the boy told you."

"I can take pills?" My stomach cramped at the thought. I'd done the severe cramps and vomiting thing twice now. I wasn't looking forward to a repeat.

"Crush one," he said. "Mix it in the blood before you drink." He nodded, making a little "hmmph" of satisfaction. "Don't they teach you kids anything in school these days?"

"Not that," I said.

"And not Latin, either, I'm guessing," he said, holding out his hand. "Let's see the document."

He'd changed the conversation so fast that I handed it over without sticking up for my skills in Latin—which were A+ quality, thank you very much!

He opened the sheet, then settled in the ratty recliner. I got up off the couch so I could stand beside him as he unfolded the paper.

The print was old-fashioned. That annoying calligraphy that makes it so hard to read documents like the Declaration of Independence and the Gutenberg Bible and stuff. I made out a few words—sun, freedom, night—but I wasn't exactly zooming along. It wasn't just the handwriting, either. A lot of the words were unfamiliar, and the endings and stems that had been so familiar on our last pop quiz now looked like a bunch of squiggles.

Apparently an A+ in second-semester Latin isn't all that useful in the real world.

I was about to say that we needed to carefully type it up so that we could look at it with a dictionary handy when Grandpa Greene started reading.

"Draw close, dark apprentice," he read, *"and learn the truth. The path out of the darkness and into the freedom of the sun has been forged."* He frowned. "Or maybe that means 'paved,' I'm not quite sure." A quick shake of his head, and he was off again, his finger moving over the document as he squinted through narrow half-glasses. *"The secret rests with the first of us, whose blood intoxicates as wine, yet holds the truth for he who would reveal it. Ancestor and heir, self and same. We crave the secret and seek the knowledge. Locate the talisman and gather the light. To you, dark apprentice, I assign these tasks. Lift the night, and free us all."*

Arvin looked up. "That's it. That's all it says."

I looked at Clayton, then Jenny. They both shrugged, clearly as befuddled as I felt. ·

"Um," I finally managed. "So?"

"So obviously," Arvin said, handing me the paper and then pushing himself out of his seat, "this Stephen character thinks you can figure out the spell that's going to let all you vampires walk around during the day."

"What?" I'd gotten really great reading comprehension scores on every standardized test I'd ever taken, but I was so not following him.

"The secret. The talisman. Some sort of spell or something for letting vampires walk in the sun." He tapped the paper I was still holding. "It's all right there, girlie. Or weren't you paying attention?"

"But . . . but . . . but!" I was sputtering, so I took a deep breath and tried again. "I can't figure that out!" I started to panic. I mean, I do okay in school. And, yes, I've won the science fair a few times. And, yes, I have a part-time job in a hospital at a medical lab. But come on! I wouldn't even know where to start!

"We'd *better* figure it out," Clayton said. "Because if you don't start making progress, Stephen may decide you're not so useful after all."

"Oh," I said, the truth of his words erasing the little flutter of happiness that his use of the pronoun "we" had caused. "Right."

"You've got more problems than that," Arvin said, and all three of us kids looked up at him. "Solve that mystery, and you'll be loosing vampires on the world. Don't, and you may find yourself erased by your master."

"Great," I said. "So glad I have options."

Arvin snorted. "Don't really see that you do. Not unless you want to stay a vampire."

"So Clayton was right? I really can turn this back. I can be me again?"

"You can," he said, then bit the end off a cigar and spat it into a corner. I wrinkled my nose but didn't say anything. "And you better do it before he decides you're no use to him. Or before you accidentally stumble across the answer to the daywalking mystery. Because you know you better look like you're searching for the solution."

"I know." I'd already thought about that. Even if I didn't *want* to find the answer, I still had to put on a good show of looking for it. "So what do I need to do?"

Arvin snorted again. "Ain't it obvious? You got to kill him."

"But I *can't* kill him," I protested. "I already told you!"

"I'll kill him for you," Clayton said, his jaw firm. "It would be my pleasure."

I turned to him, feeling all gooey inside as I tried to imagine him up on a white steed.

"You can't, boy," Arvin said. "Has to come from her."

"But I can't," I said. "I mean, I already tried. He even gave me the stake to try with!"

"You can't *stake* him," Arvin said, cutting me off. "Don't mean you can't manage to terminate the critter." He looked me dead in the eye. "You just gotta figure out how. And it's gotta come from you or else you won't turn back to one of us. Bad magic's got its rules, you know."

I shivered, unsettled by the whole bad magic thing.

"And you better figure it out soon," Jenny said. She'd been quiet through all of this, but now she looked deadly serious. "Because if Kevin or his brother kills Stephen first—"

"You'll be shit out of luck, girlie-girl."

CHAPTER 24

Arvin's revelation had totally freaked me out. But I knew he was right—even if I couldn't figure out *how* he could be right. After all, he'd been right about the Vivarin. I'd tried it about an hour before sunup, and the caffeine had given me the extra jolt of peppiness I needed to listen to the recording on my cell phone. And, let me tell you, there was some *very* interesting stuff there.

I'd been about to download it to an MP3 file and e-mail it to Jenny when Clayton had banged at my window, signaling that it was time for us to head to school. The streets were pretty deserted, and we got there in no time.

"If I fall asleep," I said as we crept into the journalism room, "you'll drag me somewhere dark and out of the way, right?" The last thing I wanted was all sorts of rumors flying about the valedictorian passed out in the journalism room.

"No problem," he said. "I'll just lock you in the dark-room."

I made a face—because it stinks in there—but saw that

he was laughing. "Okay, then," I said. "So long as you have a plan . . ."

"Do *you* have a plan?" He was looking at me with interest, and I didn't know what to tell him. There's a long cabinet in the journalism room—we use it to lay out the paper—and I pulled myself up and sat there, legs swinging in front of me.

I shook my head, frustrated. "I have to kill him. Except—"

"You *can't* kill him."

"Kind of a pickle, huh?"

He raised an eyebrow. "A *pickle*? You really are as innocent as everyone says, aren't you?"

I bared my teeth at him, trying to look anything *but* innocent. "Watch yourself, Greene. I'm not innocent anymore. I'm trouble."

And—damn him—he laughed!

After a second, I laughed, too. "Fine," I said, between giggles. "It's not a pickle. It's completely screwed up. Better?"

"Much. So what are you going to do about it?"

"I wish I knew." I yawned, then looked at Clayton with a mixture of horror and determination.

"Here," he said, quickly. "Drink."

I found a straw shoved in my face. The straw, I saw, led to one of those soft-pack water bottles, the kind that serious cyclists wear. I didn't need to ask what was in the bottle; I could smell the delicious scent already. *Blood.* Glorious blood. And, I was certain, a healthy dosage of crushed-up Vivarin.

I drank, and Clayton watched, his eyes never leaving my face. Well, almost never. Once the straw turned red, I noticed him staring at it rather than me. Can't say I blamed him. I mean, we both knew I wasn't sucking down cranberry juice.

As soon as I'd sucked the pack dry, I felt a bit perkier. Actually, I felt wired. "How much Vivarin did you put in there, anyway?"

He shrugged. "The box."

Great. I was going to be the first vampire in history to OD on caffeine pills.

"We can't risk you passing out during algebra," he said, apparently reading my mind.

I just scowled. This whole thing was totally messing with my mood. And although I'd noticed that my mood was definitely lighter in Clayton's presence (what was up with *that*?) for the most part, I was understandably grumpy. I mean, who wouldn't be? Some freaky Latin puzzle to solve and a burning desire for revenge.

"What?" Clayton asked.

I realized I was frowning, my forehead scrunched up in concentration. "I'm having a little trouble reconciling the fact that your grandpa says I have to kill Stephen with the whole vamps-can't-kill-their-masters thing."

"Yeah, that's a problem." He sighed. "I'd do it for you if I could."

"I know," I said, looking at my shoes before managing the courage to look up at him with a smile. "Thanks."

He looked so bummed that I felt all warm and tingly again. Or maybe the tingle was just the Vivarin-drenched blood working its way through my body. Either way, it felt nice. And, in case you're wondering, vamps *can* blush.

"What about the others?" he asked.

"Others?"

"The other vamps. You can't kill Stephen, but—"

"Whoa there, sport," I said. "In case you forgot, I'm supposed to be Cooperation Girl. I start killing off Stephen's friends, I have a feeling that he isn't gonna be too keen on keeping me undead. Just dead dead. Besides," I added, "if they're above me on the vamp food chain, Stephen says I can't kill them, either."

"But they could kill you."

"Thanks for reminding me."

He frowned. "So what *are* you going to do?"

I lifted the corner of my mouth in a smile—the one my mother always says makes me look like I'm up to something. Because I'd been thinking about that very thing. And about the recording on my cell phone. And about the popular kids in general.

And I finally had a plan.

Well, sort of, anyway.

CHAPTER 25

Okay, so it wasn't actually a *plan*. More like a vague idea.

Or, not even an idea, really. More like a compulsion. But, hey, compulsive people succeed, right? I mean, I've always been compulsive about my grades, and look where it got me (the valedictorian thing, not the undead thing).

Anyway, the point was, I was obsessed with the idea of revenge. I couldn't kill Stephen (or, rather, I apparently *could*, I just didn't know *how*), and I couldn't kill his little vampy cohorts.

But in high school, there are better ways to get revenge than death. I mean, reputation is everything. Especially for the Tamara-Stephen-Chris-Stacy crowd. I might not be able to whack their little undead butts, but if I could knock them down a peg or two . . . well, that would certainly make me a happy camper.

It wasn't much, but it was all I had to work with. So I went over to the computer in the corner of the journalism room and navigated over to the *Waterloo Watch* blog.

Sure enough, there was my photo of Tamara, all kissy face with Kevin's brother, her boobs practically falling out of the thin little tank top she was wearing.

The picture was posted under a huge headline: IT'S NOT PEER PRESSURE OR QUESTIONABLE VALUES IF HE'S CUTE. And then under the picture was Jenny's sarcastic little blurb comparing Tamara's various Voice of Waterloo speeches with her suck-face-a-thon in the bar.

The comments, I noticed, had topped one hundred. With six more posting between the time I logged on and the time I refreshed the screen. And the word "hypocrite" (and some other not nice words) was popping up frequently.

Oh yeah. With Tamara, reputation was everything. And hers was spiraling down.

A few people seemed to side with her, though. Including Richie Carter, which I thought was truly weird. And he was using his debate team clout to help bolster her reputation.

Not good.

Still, the picture (and the hypocrite comments) were a start. And the recording would be the icing on the cake.

Not that I had time to worry about getting the file to Jenny at the moment. The first period bell had already rung, and Clayton was gathering his backpack and shoving mine into my arms. "Smile," he demanded.

"Why?" I asked, but did as I was told.

He leaned in and inspected my teeth. "Okay. You're good. No fangs. Try to avoid getting hungry, okay? And if you need to feed go to the bathroom or something," he said as he passed me another soft pack filled with blood, glorious blood.

"I'm not an idiot," I said as I shoved the soft thermos into my book bag. But I understood his concern. My teeth were tingling just from the knowledge that I was carting around a liter or so of blood.

This vamp thing was going to take some getting used to.

"You awake?"

"Totally," I said, bolstered by the effects of a billion milligrams of caffeine.

"Don't forget to schedule time in the science lab. You're going to need it." He was right about that. Even if I could sneak in some time at the hospital lab by telling Cary, the head technician, that I was working on a school project, I still needed all the lab time I could wrangle.

"No problem," I said.

"Great." He looked at his shoes. "So, I guess I'll see you in journalism? I laid out the paper yesterday, but you need to look it over and write your editorial."

"Right." I thought about that, then frowned. The thing is, the paper was my baby, but juggling the paper, my grades, and my undead responsibilities was going to be a tough one.

"Don't worry," Clayton said, apparently reading my mind. "We're not going to let an issue slide. We have to be at school before dawn anyway. We'll get it all done."

Again with the "we." Only now, I was starting to expect it. Which, honestly, was almost as nice as actually hearing it.

We said one of those awkward good-byes, and I raced off to class, already looking forward to seeing Clayton again. My first two periods went by without a hitch. Then I saw Stacy in all her raven-haired glory, not undead. Just brain-dead.

She followed me out of government class and cornered me at my locker. "You're such a little bitch. Don't think we don't know."

"Know what?"

"The picture," she said. "On the *Watch* blog. That has to have been you." She smiled coldly. "Stephen's pissed."

"Yeah? Well, I know the feeling." If I'd had a heartbeat, it would have been doing double or triple time. Since I didn't, I was feeling calm, cool, and collected.

Hopefully, that made me a stellar liar.

"*You're* pissed?" she repeated. "What do you have to be mad about?"

"Other than the obvious?" I shot back. "Well, for starters, where do you get off accusing me of posting that photo? Do you think Richie and Tony and the rest of those kids *like* you? Any one of them could have taken that picture, and considering Stephen and Chris and Ennis are feeding off of them, I think they have one heck of a motive to post pictures on the Net."

"They don't even know what's going on," Stacy said.

"Don't be so sure," I spat. "And don't go around accusing me of doing stupid things. Believe me, pissing Stephen off would be a stupid thing. And I'm not an idiot. That's why you all wanted me, right?"

She licked her lips, and I could see she was doubting herself.

"So then who did take the picture?"

"I don't care," I said. "All I'm interested in is doing my little project for Stephen." I took a step toward her, feeling more bold than I'd ever felt in all my years of high school. "So if you'll move aside."

"You promise you didn't post that picture?"

"Cross my heart," I said. *And hope to die.* I waited a beat, then said, "I heard about Ennis. Is it true?"

She crossed her arms over her chest. "Somebody staked him."

I shivered, the idea still totally creeping me out. "I have to go," I said, just wanting to get away from her.

"You'll be at practice, though, right?"

"Yeah," I said. "I'll be there."

I grabbed my pretend lunch and headed for the cafeteria. On the way, I noticed Richie Carter and Tim Dalton. I'd seen both at the bar, and both had Band-Aids on their necks. Courtesy of the popular vamps' Dine On Our Classmates plan. But why were Richie and friends letting them do it? Honestly, it made no sense.

Not that I could concentrate. Just the thought made me hungry, and I looked longingly after a cute guy in a University of Texas T-shirt and Wranglers. And (I'm embarrassed to admit) the longing had nothing to do with how nice he looked in those tight jeans.

Ugh. Just what I needed. Vampire lust. *Not!*

I was walking backward—the better to see Wrangler boy—when I stumbled over someone. I heard a cry, then a tumble, and turned around to discover that I'd knocked Elise to the floor.

"I'm sorry!" I squealed, reaching out a hand to help her up as all the kids in the caf started laughing. "I didn't see you," I said as I tugged her to her feet.

"So I noticed," she said, her voice as cold as ice.

I flinched. "What's up?"

"You promised!"

"I what?" I mean, I hadn't even seen her in two days, and—

Oh.

"Lunch," I said, squinting as if she was going to hit me in the face. "And algebra. Oh God, Elise. I really am sorry. Something came up."

"Sure something came up," she said. "Something with Stacy and Stephen and the rest of their dumb jock friends."

"No!" I protested. Then, "Well, yeah. Sorta. But that's not why I didn't make lunch. I was—"

What? What was I?

"God, Beth, I always thought you were better than that."

"I *am* better than that!"

"Well, you've certainly got the right ego for their crowd," she said. Then she lifted her chin, spun on her heel, and started walking away.

This *so* wasn't going well.

Trouble was, the whole thing really was my fault. And even though I had way better things to worry about than Elise's midterm, I also knew that I was the one who'd screwed up here. Not that I could have helped it, but I should have remembered. Called or e-mailed or something once I made it home Tuesday night. Instead I'd blown her off. And since I couldn't explain the real reason, I could totally see how she'd be pissed at me.

She was, of course, halfway across the caf by that time. I exhaled loudly, then raced after her, finally cornering her by the lockers. "We need to talk."

"I was going to take my lunch and sit outside," she said. "It's a free country. You can come if you want to."

"Ah. Right. How 'bout we find a quiet corner somewhere?" I offered a weak smile. "Allergies."

I thought she was going to argue, but she just skulked away, finally ending up on one of the benches outside the band hall. "Good enough?"

I ignored the challenge. "Sure. Good. Great."

She crossed her arms over her chest.

"Come on, Elise. I didn't stand you up. I was home. Sick. Ask Jenny if you don't believe me. Or Clayton. He knows. He brought me some homework."

She made a snorting noise. "They'll probably say anything you want them to."

I wasn't sure what to say, especially since I realized I wasn't really concentrating on her words anymore. Instead, I was bouncing a little on my seat. That, I figured, was from the Vivarin. But the burning in my throat? *That* was from the scent of Elise.

I twisted a little, trying to get a better look at her. Sure enough, I saw a bandage on her neck. I could even see a little red stain under it. And that tiny little hint of blood was making gallons of saliva in my mouth.

"For cripes sake, Beth, *what* is your problem?"

I blinked up at her, realizing I'd totally zoned out. "I, um, told you I'd been sick. Just feeling a little woozy. That's all."

She rolled her eyes again, then reached into her purse and pulled out a couple of pills. "Iron," she said. "My doctor says I'm anemic."

Considering the Band-Aid on her neck, I wasn't too surprised. "Elise," I asked. "Are you still hanging around with Chris?"

I expected her to tell me to get a life. Instead, she blushed. "No. I mean, yes. I mean . . ." She sighed. "When I broke up with him, I was pissed, you know? But then later . . ."

"You still like him." I couldn't imagine *why* it was true, but I knew it had to be.

"He's a jerk now," she said, her chin high. "But he didn't use to be. And so I . . . well, I . . ."

"Stalk him?" I suggested, helpfully.

"Something like that," she mumbled, looking at her sandwich rather than her hands.

"Stay clear of him," I said, thinking about her neck. "He's bad news. They all are."

She lifted an eyebrow. "You'd do good to take your own advice."

Yeah, I thought. *I would.*

CHAPTER 26

One of the benefits of being the smart girl in school is the opportunity to take a lot of independent study courses during junior and senior year. I have journalism right after lunch (during which I spent equal time working on the paper and sneaking glances at Clayton). Then the rest of the day I'm pretty much on my own. On Thursdays, I have Independent Study Literature right next to Independent Study Chemistry. And *that* meant that I could totally blow off English and spend a full two hours in the chemistry lab. (And, no, this wouldn't raise any sort of red flags with the faculty. I meet with my advisor, Ms. Ralston, after school on Fridays to discuss my progress on my term paper. On Tuesdays and Thursdays—my official class time—she's teaching grammar to the ninth-graders. I get a hall pass, a pat on the head, and the run of the school.)

With grades comes freedom. That's my motto . . .

At any rate, as it turned out, I was the only one in the

chemistry lab. (The other independent study kids are Jake Procter and Candy Matheson, and since they started going out, they tend to spend a lot of time "studying" in the backseat of Jake's Beemer.) This was good news for me. Not only could I play my music (Train) as loud as I wanted, I could poke around and try to figure out my freaky Latin puzzle in peace.

The Latin copy was still at my house, hidden in my underwear drawer just in case my mom caught some rare virus and decided to suddenly take an interest in my life. I had the translation with me, though, and I was determined to make some headway. Chemistry, physics, history. I didn't care. I was looking at it all.

Biology first. I figured that made sense, after all, since the message talked about the blood holding the truth "for he who would reveal it." Or she, I thought, as I stabbed my forefinger with a pin.

Jenny walked in just as I did that. "Ouch! What are you doing?"

"Experimenting," I said, squeezing a drop of my blood into a test tube. "Run next door and ask Mr. Jordan if I can borrow a microscope." I didn't hear her feet move, so I looked up, only to find her staring at me, one eyebrow raised and her arms crossed over her chest. "Please?" I added.

That made her happy, and she cut through the shared office space into the biology teacher's room. I knew class was going on, but I also knew that Mr. Jordan lectured on Mondays, then gave out worksheets for the rest of the week. Which meant he was probably drinking coffee in the office area and Jenny should be returning right about . . .

Now.

"Got it," she said, coming back in with one of the smaller microscopes. "Will this do?"

"We'll see."

While I set it up, Jenny went back for slides. When she returned, I smeared some of my blood on one and popped the slide onto the plate.

"What are you looking for?" she asked.

"I have no idea." I mean, I'm smart, but I'm not *that* smart. And my blood looked like . . . well, *blood*. Maybe I could see a difference with the lab equipment, but under the microscope, it just looked like blood.

I looked up to face Jenny. "Give me some of yours."

"Excuse me?"

"Hold out your finger," I said wearily, brandishing a straight pin.

"No way." She backed away, her finger held tight to her chest. "No way, no how, no go."

"Don't be such a baby. It's only a prick."

"It's *blood*, Beth. As soon as you prick me, you're going to go all fangy on me. And don't even say you aren't, because you know it's true."

Okay, maybe she had a little bit of a point there.

"Go do it outside and bring me back the slide."

She gave me one of *those* looks, but I just shooed her out. She snatched the pin out of my hand and went. A minute or so later, she was back. "Here."

I took it and compared her blood to mine. "I don't see a thing," I said.

"Nothing?"

"Nothing at all."

"You didn't think it would be that easy, did you?" Stephen's deep voice filled the room, and Jenny and I sprang to attention. "Our blood is not the key to the riddle. In fact, it very clearly speaks of the master's blood."

"Thanks for the input," I said snippily. "But from what I understand of vampires, we all have a little bit of the master's blood."

He moved toward me even as I moved backward, until I found myself smooshed up against the hard edge of a lab desk. "Believe me, Elizabeth," he said, stroking his finger down my neck. "You don't know half as much about vampires as you think you do."

I sucked in air, fighting to keep from shaking. Mostly in rage, but, yes, a little bit in lust, too. Even now that I knew he was Evil Incarnate, I still had to admit that he was pretty dang hot. "If there are things I need to know," I finally said, "then maybe you should tell me. Otherwise, I doubt I'm going to be much help."

"And deny you the joy of learning? Elizabeth, I wouldn't dream of it."

And then, in an instant, he was gone. Moving so fast I could barely see him leave. I swear, if he'd had a black cape, he would have flipped it in my face.

"*What* was that?" Jenny asked, her eyes wide.

"My master," I said dryly. "Or hadn't you heard?"

CHAPTER 27

I didn't give up entirely on the blood thing, but I will admit that Stephen's little speech had taken the bloom off my research efforts. Scientifically, at least. Before I left school, I used the library's computer to make a list of all the books I could find about vampire lore, the origins of vampires, and all the oh-so-fascinating rest of it.

Hollywood may say that Dracula was the first vampire, but I wasn't so sure. And since the Latin riddle talked about a talisman, I figured I needed to know who I was dealing with. I mean, maybe there was a traveling museum exhibit, and I just needed to commit a minor felony in order to get the thing that would save me. That would be okay, right? I mean, I was already dead. How much worse could jail be?

The one incredibly useful fact I did learn was all about glamour. Not the Hollywood kind. The vampire kind.

That was when it all clicked. The way Stephen had sucked me in before he'd turned me. It hadn't been lust—it had been *glamour*. In other words, magic. A spell. And once he'd vamped me, the spell was broken, and I saw the real Stephen loud and clear.

I didn't get to do too much more research, though, because I had to go play cheerleader at exactly six-thirty-six (which, in case you're wondering, is one minute after sunset).

Oh, the joy.

I was heading out of the library—a stack of books shoved under my arms—when I bumped into Richie Carter.

Splat!

All my books went flying.

I threw myself down and started gathering them up.

"A little light reading?" he asked, holding up *The Vampire Book*, a huge encyclopedia of vampire lore.

"Writing a script," I said. "You know. To go with my film school application." That actually wasn't such a bad idea, and I made a mental note to consider that very thing. Assuming I ever got back to the land of the living.

"Oh. Good idea." He'd stacked them up and now he handed them to me. Then he got to his feet and started walking away. "Well, see you."

"Richie!"

He stopped, and I realized I didn't have a clue what to say. "How come you were at that club last night?"

He looked away, his face going pink. "Why were you?"

"Cheerleading," I said. "It seems I don't have a choice."

"Guess we're even, then. Tamara asked me."

"And you went? She doesn't even like you."

He lifted a shoulder. "She's not that bad. I mean, maybe she doesn't want to hang out during school, but she's okay."

"She just wants your vote," I said.

"She'd probably be good," he said.

"What did you do at the club?" I asked, changing tacks. "I mean, did you hang with her?"

"Not really," he said. "But, you know, we had fun."

"What happened to your neck?"

His hand lifted automatically to the sore. "No idea. Woke up with the bandage on. Guess I scratched it in my sleep and forgot about it."

"Mmmm," I said, as the word *glamour!* flashed neon in my mind.

"What's that supposed to mean?"

"Do me a favor, okay? Just pay attention. Tamara's got an agenda. And I really think she's using you."

"Maybe I'm using her right back," he said.

And, you know? He probably was. I mean, isn't the definition of high school all about using people in order to fight your way up some stupid social hierarchy (am I jaded, or what?)? But Tamara had the advantage—she knew about the vamps. And Richie was just a meal ticket to her.

I hoped I'd at least hinted heavily enough that he'd pay attention (and read the *Watch*!) but I didn't have time to worry about it since I was already late for practice.

I found Tamara, Stacy, and the rest of the gang on the field, all decked out in their little uniforms. All except for Melissa, who was sitting cross-legged in the grass, faded mascara lines marking her face.

The other girls were doing a good job of ignoring her. Stacy, as usual, had a hairbrush in one hand and was doing the requisite one hundred strokes.

I resisted the urge to roll my eyes.

I also resisted the urge to grab hold of a few locks and tug. Hard.

"Beth!"

I jerked my chin up and found myself facing Tamara. "What?"

"*Where* is your head? I've been calling and calling." I waited for her to say something about the *Watch* photo, but nothing came. Maybe I'd managed to convince Stacy of my innocence earlier.

"Beth!"

"Sorry!" I plastered on a simpering grin. "I was just admiring Stacy's hair."

"Too bad yours is so shaggy," Stacy retorted, her smile sweeter than divinity. "Now that you've been vamped, you're stuck with what you've got. Too bad you hadn't made a trip to Supercuts recently." Her pert little nose wrinkled, and I fought the urge to rip it off. "Must be hell knowing you have to go through eternity looking like *that*."

I bit my lip. Not because I was pissed (I was), but because she was right. I desperately needed highlights and a cut, but unless I wanted to deal with that every morning for the rest of my un-life, there was no point. Apparently all those books and movies about vampires got it right: you keep the looks you had when you died. So even if I bothered to do an early evening salon thing every day (night?), I'd be back to the same old dark roots and uneven bob the next night.

Did my luck suck, or what?

"When *I'm* vamped," Lisa said, "I'm going to make sure it's after I've just been to the salon. Maybe fly to Beverly Hills or something."

I didn't bother pointing out that the plan seemed a little extreme. I was too busy cluing in to the big bomb Lisa had dropped. "What do you mean, when *you're* vamped?"

Her eyes went wide, and Tamara kicked her in the shin.

"God, Lis," Stacy said, her tone bored even though she was obviously leery. "Do you have some sort of learning deficiency? Some sort of chemical imbalance that makes it impossible for you to keep your mouth shut?"

"*Sor*-ry!"

Joan rolled her eyes. "Lay off her, Stace. It's not that big a deal anymore. I mean, she's hardly out of the loop now."

"That's right," I said. "I'm in the loop." I stared at them. "So what loop?"

Eye to eye to eye until finally they made a decision. "We wanted to have done it by now," Tamara said. "But that kind of screwed up the early games and car washes and stuff."

"Do it," I repeated. "You mean turn into vampires?" Oh, *man*. I'd figured out they were Renfields, but I just assumed they got a kick out of dating the undead boys. Like maybe they thought it was a step above dating a jock. But they actually *wanted* this?

"It's pathetic that you've got it before any of us," Tamara said. "I mean, look at you."

I ignored the insult. "Early games and car washes. No way you can do that."

"Touché," Tamara said.

"And you want to do this why?" Honestly, considering how much Tamara liked the look of herself in a bikini, I really couldn't imagine.

"Cheer competition," she said. "I mean, duh."

"Oh." I tried to process that. "Um . . ."

She rolled her eyes. "As soon as you figure out the secret for staying out during the day without looking like a damn minstrel, then the whole squad can convert."

"Convert?" I mimicked. "Not exactly the word I'd use."

"Honestly, I don't care what word you'd use," Tamara

said. "So long as you figure out how vamps can walk during the day before the time change comes again . . ."

"Oh, sure. That's what I live for. Solving your problems."

"Please," Tamara said. "You don't think Stephen actually *likes* you, do you? He didn't even let you drink from his neck, did he?"

I frowned, remembering how I drank from a glass. "So wha—?"

"I drink from his neck. Every day." She licked her lips, slow and sensuous. Like a model or something. "Delicious."

"You do what? Why?"

"Why the hell do you think?"

I had no clue, but I didn't have a chance to press the point because suddenly Melissa wasn't comatose anymore. No, suddenly she was on her feet, tears streaming down her face. "How can you guys even think about that anymore! I mean look what happened! Doesn't anybody care? He's *dead*!"

"Well, duh," Tamara said. "He's been dead for months."

Melissa licked her lips. "I don't wanna die. Not like that."

"We aren't going to," Tamara said, shooting a look my way. "We're just going to win."

"Not if we don't get on with practice." Stacy stood to one side, tapping her foot, and shooting killer glances toward Melissa.

"Right." Tamara looked at all the girls. "Everyone have a power drink today? Everyone except Beth, that is? She's got the real thing."

"You are such a bitch!" Melissa yelled, then slapped Tamara square across the face. Then she took off running. And that girl ran *fast*.

"Let her go," Stacy said, as Tamara yelped. "She's just upset about Ennis. Derek offered her a drink, but she blew him off. She'll come around."

"She'd better," Tamara said, coldly. Then she sighed. "Come on. Let's get to work."

"Ladies! Ladies!" That from Ladybell, who'd been across the field working with two dozen drill team girls. Now she was rushing toward us, her hand waving. "Is there a problem?"

Tamara shook her head. "No, ma'am. No problem."

Ladybell looked around, clearly counting. "And where is your sixth? This team can't drop below six. I've cut down to the slimmest, most efficient number possible, but I can't cut any further!" Her voice was rising, almost hysterical, and I was trying really hard not to roll my eyes. This was a woman who took cheerleading just a little too seriously.

Then again, the girls were drinking vampire blood to get an edge. So maybe they fit right in after all.

"Melissa's not feeling well. No biggie."

"You're certain? We need to get these routines nailed."

"Positive," Stacy said.

Ladybell looked to each of us, and I managed a forced smile when her eyes landed on me. "I hope you're as good as I think you are," she said.

"Yes, ma'am," I said. Which was stupid, but I couldn't think what else to say.

"Very well. And remember, I want all of you at the basketball tryouts on Monday. I expect a flawless routine."

"Yes, ma'am." And this time, that came from all of us.

Then she turned, flipped her hair, and headed back across the field toward the drill team.

"Isn't she going to coach us?"

Tamara rolled her eyes. "We're doing just fine." She motioned to the field. "Come on, ladies. Let's show little Bethie the routine."

I blanched as Tamara, Joan, Stacy, and Lisa leaped into the air, doing kick-ass, damn-near-perfect backflips onto the field. Not an impossible move, mind you, but I've known these girls for years. Dancers, yes. Gymnasts, no.

Now, though, they'd probably take the gold in the floor exercises.

And I could think of only one explanation. Not steroids. That was waaaaaay too passé.

No, my squadmates were loading up on vampire blood.

Personally, I think they were taking the competitive edge a little too far.

CHAPTER 28

Friday was weird.

Okay, that's probably an understatement in light of everything that had happened to me. But it really was. Weird, I mean.

But weird in a good way.

Or, it didn't start out good, but then it turned good. After it turned bad, I mean.

But it was mostly good. And even the bad was good. Probably.

I think.

Okay, rewind. The whole thing started right before first period. In the halls. With lots of whispering and finger-pointing. Not at me, but at Tamara. Because Jenny had posted the MP3 file to the *Watch* blog. Apparently someone had taken offense, and wanted to share the outrage. They'd made up a flyer and left stacks all over the hallways.

I picked one up.

IS THIS THE VOICE WE WANT?
Tamara McKnight, the Voice of Vitriol
Check it out at http://thewaterloowatch.blogspot.com
And vote no!

The paper held no clue as to exactly what vitriol Tamara was spouting (that was okay, though, because you only had to listen in on the gossip for three seconds to figure it out). I didn't have to listen, though. I knew. After all, I'd made the recording.

"This totally sucks. Slumming with the likes of Richie and Danielle and the rest of these dweebs," she'd said. "I mean, save me from a life with the dull and slow-witted."

She'd been talking with Stephen, so there was a lot more there. Stuff that gave away the whole vampire thing. I'd actually considered posting that, too, but decided against it. It was a trump card if I needed it, but I didn't think I would.

This morning, I'd checked on the *Waterloo Watch*, and Tamara had slipped in the Voice polls. Stephen was still up there (I didn't have a tape of him—not yet, anyway), but *I* was actually higher than Tamara. Which was particularly funny since Jenny had only put me on as a joke.

Anyway, that's how the day started out good. It got weird (and bad) once I got to the lab. After first period, I made excuses to all of my teachers so that I got to cut classes and go work on my fictitious science fair project.

As for my real project, I wasn't making any progress, because I'm not Albert Einstein or Madame Curie, and Stephen's an idiot if he thinks I'm going to figure this thing out. (I mean, I am *so* screwed!) For about five seconds I'd considered asking my dad to take a look at my blood and tell me if he saw anything freaky weird, but then I realized that was a totally insane idea. What could

I say? "Here, Dad, I'm a vampire, and I'm trying to find a cure"?

Um, no.

Which left me to do the work myself.

At any rate, there I was, analyzing the chemical components of vitamin D because UV light induces the production of vitamin D, so I figured it was worth a shot—maybe vampires are allergic to vitamin D and it's not about the blood at all? It was a half-decent theory. Half because I wasn't sure about the vitamin D part, but I *knew* UV light was part of the problem. I knew this because I'd put a UV lightbulb in a box yesterday, wired it up, then stuck my finger inside. I'd burned the hell out of the finger, screamed bloody murder, then patted myself on the back for being such a dedicated scientist.

And, fortunately for me, my crispy critter finger was whole again after I slept. All thanks to the wonders of vampiric blood.

At any rate, I was certain that the UV component of light was key somehow, I just wasn't sure how. And I was making no headway whatsoever.

I had my head bent over a lab table, a beaker bubbling in front of me, and my plastic goggles on, out of habit.

That's when Derek walked in.

"You," he said, a finger pointed toward me and his face contorted.

I took a step backward, my hands up. "Whoa, Derek. What's up?"

"Nothing's up. *You're* down." He poked me in the chest. "You are *so* going down."

"Get a grip. I haven't done anything to you."

"No? What about what you did to Ennis? What about—"

"I didn't do anything to Ennis!"

But he wasn't listening. "And Tamara!" he yelled. "You know what's going to happen to us if those little jerks stop coming to the bar? What are we supposed to do then? And Stephen thinks you're some great hope? You're just stuck-up. That's what you are. A stuck-up little princess who thinks she's smarter than everyone else."

He'd backed me into a corner, and he'd brought a glass beaker with him. Now he smashed it against the side of the lab table and rushed me. I yelped and cowered, but it didn't do any good. The glass came down, slicing my shoulder and sending pain searing through me.

The smell of blood filled the air, making me hungry even though I knew it was my own. I yelped and tried to move backward, but I was as far back as I could go.

"I don't care what Stephen says. You're going to ruin it for all of us!"

"But I didn't—"

"Shut up!"

I shut up. I mean, he obviously didn't believe me. And I was pretty much lying anyway.

"Just because I can't kill you doesn't mean I can't make it bad for you," he said. "How'd you like to be alive in little pieces, scattered all over Zilker Park?"

"Derek, come on! You don't really want to—"

"Oh, I think I do."

And then he lunged again, only this time he had a knife, and I screamed and—

Oh. My. God.

Suddenly he was a big cloud of ash fluttering in the air, and then falling to the ground. I blinked, terrified and relieved and I don't know what else.

And there, standing right in front of me, was Clayton, holding a wooden stake.

"Oh gosh, oh gosh, oh gosh!" I started to run to Clayton, realized I'd have to run over Derek's remains, and ended up sort of standing there. "He was going to rip me to shreds!"

"I know," Clayton said, slipping the stake in his back pocket—it was a totally cool maneuver—and sidestepping Derek. Then he held on to my uninjured shoulder. I sort of stood there, kind of trembly, and still not entirely sure what happened. "You okay?"

I nodded. "I think. I mean, yes. I mean . . . thank you." I was barely whispering. And I was looking right at him. And when I saw him leaning in, I actually held my breath even though I wasn't, you know, actually breathing.

And then he kissed me. (Which was the good part, in case you're wondering.) And then Mr. Jordan opened the door, and we both jumped.

"I thought I heard a crash," he said.

"Um, yeah," I said. "I dropped a beaker."

"Hmmm." He looked at Clayton. "Don't you have a class, Mr. Greene?"

"Yeah," he said. Then he held up a laminated card. "But I had to talk to Beth. And I have a hall pass."

"Finish up," Mr. Jordan said. He started to leave, then paused, eyeing both of us. "And leave the door open."

My cheeks flamed, and if I'd drunk any more blood that day, I swear I would have been bright red. I took a step back, rubbing my palms on my jeans out of habit. Vampires, it appeared, didn't get sweaty palms.

"Um, so, what are we going to do?" I asked.

"About what?"

"About what?! About Derek!"

He glanced at the dust. "You didn't see him. I didn't see him." He hooked a finger under my chin. "You got it?"

"I got it."

He started toward the door, then he stopped and turned back to me. "He was already dead, you know. There wasn't any coming back for him."

I stifled a shiver.

"We're getting you back," he said with a smile that left me all tingly again. "And I'll stake anybody that tries to stop us."

And that part was good, too.

My whole situation, though . . . this whole vampire thing? Well, it was still very, very bad.

CHAPTER 29

"So you like him, then?" The question came from Jenny. At the moment, we were crouched in the bushes outside Stacy's house, and although gossiping about boys sounded like a heavenly little slice of normalcy, I was thinking that maybe now wasn't the time.

"Beth?" she pressed.

I put a finger to my lips and pointed to Stacy's window. "Shhhhh." I'd told Jenny about the whole thing—Derek and Clayton and what had come after. The kiss, I mean. And about how he'd walked with me after school (as in, after sundown after school). And we'd held hands. It felt wild and crazy and decadent . . . and normal.

And I liked that. Especially after the decidedly non-normal afternoon. I mean, I've seen a lot of stuff. But a vampire exploding in front of me? That was a new one.

And maybe I did want to talk about it . . . because there really was a lot of stuff just going round and round in my head. But not now. Not in the middle of Mission Shear Stacy.

"We are going to get *so* busted," Jenny said, as I raised up on my toes to peer in through Stacy's window. "Or, rather, *I'm* going to get so busted, since you can't even go inside!"

I shrugged sheepishly. Because she was right. I needed help with this one. But in the end, it would be *so* worth it.

I tested the window sash. "Unlocked," I said. Apparently Stacy was as bad as me about locking up her room.

"You're sure she won't wake up?"

"Positive," I said. "But, you know, be careful anyway. And quiet."

Jenny stared at me, but didn't move.

"It'll be fine," I said. "I cornered Melissa and chatted her up. The blood they drink makes them strong for a while, but then it wipes them out. Trust me. Stacy is sleeping like a rock." I slowly opened the window the rest of the way. "So you know what to do?" I whispered.

Jenny took a breath, then stood. She held up the scissors, their steel edge gleaming in the moonlight. "I know," she said.

And then she slipped inside.

CHAPTER 30

I spent most of the weekend (well, the weekend nights) at the hospital being Super Research Girl. Since the hospital lab was officially my part-time weekend employer, there was nothing weird about my camping out there. And since my boss, Cary, thinks that I'm the most responsible teenager ever, destined to graduate at the top of my med school class (he's been listening to my dad), he was more than willing to let me stick around after I clocked out and work on my "science project." And since my mother was still preparing for trial, she didn't care if I was out at all hours. Yet another benefit of being smart and well behaved: adults never assume you've been turned into a vampire against your will.

At any rate, on the whole, the weekend was perfect. Minimal parental contact. Minimal vampiric activity. Minimal hunger thanks to easily accessible bags of blood. (That, yes, I stole. So sue me.) The only downside? Minimal contact with Jenny and Clayton. But their families are normal and wanted to do the quality-time thing. Since arousing parental suspicions wasn't high on our list—and since I had plenty of research to do—we decided not to push it.

All of which is why I spent the entire weekend in a state of supreme scientific activity. Which is also the reason I was in such a bad mood when Monday morning rolled around. Because I'd wasted two entire days (well, *nights*), and hadn't learned a thing.

"Nothing?" Clayton asked, when I relayed all of that to him from my little perch in the chemistry lab. "If you weren't getting anywhere, then why did you keep up the charade?"

"Because the answer's here somewhere," I said, waving at a slide smeared with my blood. I'd pretty much blown off my morning classes again, telling all of my teachers that I was in the middle of a potential science fair breakthrough. The ruse had worked and, although I was happy to have so much freedom, I had to wonder about the state of public education when no one much seemed to care if I bothered going to classes.

I made a mental note to write an editorial for the *Liberator* and kept focusing on the slide. "Something," I said. "I'm missing something big."

"Where?" Clayton asked. "In your blood? If it's there, you would have found it. You're smart, remember? That's what you're always telling me."

I made a face, then moved aside so he could look through the microscope. "You're always telling me that *you're* smart. See if you can find something."

He looked through the eyepiece, adjusted his focus, then grunted. "What am I looking for?"

"Don't know," I admitted. "I ran a zillion different tests at the hospital. The lab techs like me," I explained, in response to his querying look. "But I didn't find anything in the makeup, the chromosomes, nothing."

"So it's not the blood."

"It has to be the blood," I said, then explained about the cheerleaders' little trick to increase their athletic prowess. "They drink the blood and suddenly they're uber-cheerleaders. So what else could it be?"

I could tell from his expression he was stumped.

"Stephen's wrong," I said for emphasis. "It's in the blood. Some sort of UV–vitamin D thing. The key is right there on that slide."

"Wow," a voice from behind me said. "You really are as smart as Stephen said."

I whirled around to face Chris, who was leaning against the doorway.

"Or am I interrupting?" he said, aiming a significant look toward Clayton.

"What do you want? Or is Stephen sending his little minions to check on me?" I added nastily.

"I'm not a minion," he said. "And I came for that." He pointed toward the microscope.

"It's not—" Clayton began.

"I'm only giving it to Stephen," I said, even louder as I shot Clayton a look that I hoped he would interpret as *keep your mouth shut!*

Since he shut his mouth and turned back to the microscope, I guess it worked.

"So you've really got it?" Chris asked, coming all the way into the lab and shutting the door behind him. "You figured out how we can walk outside?"

"Stephen knew I would," I said, staring him straight in the eye and daring him to call my bluff. "That's why he picked me, right?" I kept staring. That's the trick about lying—always look them in the eye.

Beside me, I heard Clayton shift, and I prayed he wasn't

going to stand up straight and ask me what I was talking about.

"So fork it over." He held out his hand.

I swallowed. "To you? No way. Send Stephen."

"He's busy. I'm second in command. Or hadn't you heard?"

I hadn't, actually, but probably best for Chris's ego (and my overall safety) not to mention that. "He can come later," I said. "After school. It's not ready yet, anyway. There are still some, um, modifications."

Can I lay it on thick, or what?

I held my breath, wondering if Chris would buy it. "What modifications?" he asked.

"Ah, well, I have to utilize the hemoglobin and plate-let nuclei in order to bond with oxybenzone and other benzophenones in order to create not an SPF but an SFF that meets or exceeds one hundred percent." Believe it or not, I made all that up on the spur of the moment. Frankly, I think I did a kick-ass job of making up a total line of crap.

From the expressions on Clayton's and Chris's faces, the crap sounded good, too.

Clayton stayed silent (thank goodness), but Chris nod-ded. "Well, okay then. So long as you've got it under con-trol."

"And if you'd leave," I said sharply, "I can get back to work. I can't concentrate with you hovering."

"Yeah. Right. Sure."

"Tell Stephen to come here at four. I should be back from the gym by then."

He didn't say anything, but he nodded. Then he opened the door and slipped out.

"What—"

I held a finger up to my lips before Clayton could go on, then marched across the room and pulled the door shut.

"—are you doing?" he finished. "You don't know a thing! And what was all that garbage about oxybenzone? You're going to give Stephen *sunscreen*?"

I lifted a shoulder. "He doesn't know it's sunscreen. You saw Chris. I threw out a few chemical names and his eyes practically glazed over."

"Stephen is smarter than Chris," Clayton pointed out.

That was true. But I figured I could bullshit my way through this. Or, at least, I hoped I could.

The thing was, I really wanted to try. Because if I could convince Stephen that this stuff would let him walk in the sun . . . and if he actually *did* walk in the sun . . . well, then I think I would have solved my little problem of how to kill my master without actually laying a hand on him.

And wouldn't that just make my entire semester?

At any rate, right then, I didn't have time to worry about it. Because even though I'd snagged lab time for the whole day, at the moment, I had to go to basketball tryouts.

I think I've already mentioned that football is king in Texas. And that's true. But once football season is over, the crown prince of basketball takes over, and most of the football gods put on their basketball god hats. And in that nether-period between football and basketball, the players try out for the team. Honestly, though, I'm not entirely sure why any of them have to audition. As far as I can tell, all the same guys make the team every year.

At any rate, because I was now a cheerleader (rah-rah!), I got to go to my first-ever basketball tryout. And the weird thing? This one, I wanted to go to.

Wanted to go so much, in fact, that I raced the whole way to the locker room, climbed eagerly into my little (and

I do mean little!) outfit, and bounced around a bit, waiting for the other girls to show up.

Or—to be more precise—waited for Stacy to show up. Which she didn't. Which totally made me giddy, especially when Ladybell arrived and started counting us off.

"And where are Melissa and Stacy?" She looked at all of us, but we shrugged. And when she turned her blue-shadowed eyes to Tamara, our fearless head cheerleader just about lost it.

"How am I supposed to know? Do you think I'm their freaking mother?"

Ladybell's eyebrows rose, and I wondered if Tamara's outburst was going to wreak havoc with her delicate sensibilities. But I'd misjudged Ladybell. She laid into Tamara hard; I swear my eyebrows were going to catch fire.

"You, missy, are the head cheerleader. Which means that you're in charge of making sure your cheerleaders are in place and ready to go at the appropriate time. Is that clear?"

I saw Tamara's eyes go wide, and then she swallowed. I also saw that look she gets when she's really, really pissed. I waited for the explosion, but it didn't come. Instead, she just nodded and said, "Yes, Ladybell."

Wow. I guess our little Tamara's growing up.

Anyway, once our fearless leader had been thoroughly chastised, we all got our pom-poms pomming and jogged out into the gym. I was behind Lisa, and I was cribbing from her like crazy. I mean, I'd only had one practice with them, and it wasn't like I had a lot of experience as an audience member to draw from. I'd avoided football and basketball games like the plague. And cheerleaders even more.

As Jenny would say, my proletariat sensibilities had come back to haunt me.

Even so, I was managing to do a decent job. I didn't

mess up a routine, and I was cheering with gusto. This, I thought, was good.

Right about the time we finished our little "We've got spirit!" rallying cry, I saw Stacy come in from the side. My eyes went wide, and I knew that if she was looking my way, my reaction was going to look *totally* genuine. I mean, the girl was practically bald! Jenny had totally *G.I. Jane*'d her!

A whole chorus of jeers went up from the bleachers, and what made my nonpopular little heart go pitter-pat was the fact that the jeers were at least as loud as the catcalls had been earlier for Tamara when we'd bounced into the gymnasium.

Yup. I might be a vampire, but at the moment I was feeling pretty good about the way I'd brought down the popularity factor of Waterloo's two Queen Bitches. Unless I missed my guess, they'd both be nearing rock bottom on tomorrow's *Waterloo Watch* poll.

Honestly, it just goes to show you, the higher up the popularity food chain you are, the further you have to fall.

At any rate, Stacy didn't look happy, but she did look . . . well, *good*. I mean, I was used to her long thick hair, but this actually looked chic.

Great. I implement a scathing plan for personalized punishment, and she comes out looking like a model for *Vogue*.

I was contemplating the unfairness of it all—and shaking my pom-poms at appropriate places—when America's Next Top Model sidled up to me. "I know you did this."

"Did what? Your hair? Are you on drugs? Is that why you're late?"

"I'm late because I had to get a salon appointment, you freak. And don't play all innocent on me. This is you. All of it. And somehow, I'm going to prove it."

"I don't know what you're talking about. Unlike some people, I have a life other than my hair. Other than *your* hair, too, for that matter. And I really wouldn't waste my time."

Okay, *that* was a major lie. But she didn't call me on it. Instead, all she did was look me straight in the eye and say, "Life? Sweetie, I think you're mistaken. *You* don't have a life."

Ouch. Okay, the girl had a point.

"But if I do find out that you did this to me," she said, leaning in close, "you're going to wish you really were dead. Because undead is going to be so not good enough to keep you safe from me."

"Hey, dude," I said, backing up with my hands up in surrender. "I told you, it wasn't me." But even as I was trying to convince her I was totally innocent, my insides were doing a victory dance. Because this was one less vampire in the halls of Waterloo.

It would be years before Stacy's hair grew out. And if I knew anything for certain, I knew that she wouldn't do the undead thing until she had at least eight inches, a Fekkai cut, and highlights.

CHAPTER 31

In case you're wondering, basketball tryouts go on forever. I mean, *forever.* Eternity as a vampire is nothing compared to how long this stuff lasts.

The student spectators are allowed to come and go as they please (along with the public, including all those coveted college scouts). But we cheerleaders have to stay through the whole freakin' fiasco. And we have to be peppy, too.

Honestly, I think that's asking just a little much.

Fortunately, though, I wasn't stuck by myself. I had my cheery cohorts (hahaha) and my partners in crime. Jenny and Clayton, to be specific. And they were armed and dangerous. Armed with holy water, and dangerous to vampires, that is.

Even Elise was there, tucked away on the bleachers, her eyes never leaving Chris. Honestly, I had no idea what she still saw in him!

Coach Dunne blew his whistle, and a bunch of guys on the court left, replaced with another bunch of guys, including Nelson and Chris. Stephen, apparently, was already on the team. He was standing with the coach, whispering things and pointing at the various guys. I wanted to fill up a spray bottle of holy water and blast him in the face. But considering the audience we had, I figured that probably wasn't such a great idea.

Another shrill whistle, and off the guys went, with Nelson and Chris jamming all over the court. Why wouldn't they? I mean, they're preternaturally fast, right?

I only hoped Clayton and Jenny could work a little magic of their own.

Tamara started making *rah-rah* noises, so I picked up the pom-pom action, yelling things like "go!" and "you can do it!" and some other cheery stuff so that it would seem like I cared. Mostly, I was watching Clayton, who was easing over toward where a few guys were warming the benches. And where a few extra balls were sitting in a tub, just waiting to be tossed into play if somebody threw a foul.

I held my breath, waiting for the opportunity for Clayton to throw a new ball in. He must have realized I was watching, though, because he looked up and smiled at me.

Okay, I was so not used to that yet. I got all tingly, my cheeks warmed, and I had to look away.

And that's when I saw him.

Kevin, my friendly neighborhood vampire hunter.

I tried to signal for Clayton, but it was too late. He was already tossing the ball in . . . and Nelson was already grabbing for it.

He reached out, ready to take the pass, and then suddenly he screeched. He fumbled (or whatever the word is for basketball) and the ball bounced away.

"What's wrong with you?" Coach shouted. "You got butter on your hands?"

"No, sir! I—" But he didn't bother finishing, just chased after the ball, then tried to dribble it again. I saw his face contort in pain and then he pushed the ball away. Not a dribble, but a shove.

Chris took up the slack, running in and accepting the pass (or whatever you could call the wildly bouncing ball), but then he fumbled, too. The whole thing was the Three Stooges on crack, and I was having a hard time not falling over with laughter.

Coach blasted out on his whistle again, and I searched the stands for Jenny and Clayton. I found them, finally, tucked into a corner, laughing so hard I was sure they were going to hurt themselves.

And the best part? Randy, my sports editor, stood front and center with his camera.

The not-so-best part? Kevin's eyes weren't glued on the court. Instead, he was looking straight at me.

CHAPTER 32

Okay, so the holy water on the basketball thing was great, but what came after was even better. After the tryouts, Coach called Nelson and Chris aside, which worked out well, because that meant that they were late getting back to the locker rooms. And that meant that all the other players had already showered and gone home.

They finally popped into the locker room, sweaty and humiliated. I wasn't supposed to be in there (duh!) but Jenny and I couldn't stand the suspense. So we hid in a corner and watched as Clayton sneaked through the room and grabbed their clothes while they were in the shower.

Jenny and I couldn't see them (which I counted as a good thing) but as soon as they finished, we knew about it.

"Hey!" Nelson said, then let up with a string of curses. "Where're my damn clothes!"

Clayton had made his way back to us, and we three crouched in the corner, trying hard to be invisible even while

I kept my phone out and ready to snap pictures if they wandered our direction in all their naked glory.

And the beautiful part? I knew that unless they were going to stay naked in the locker room until sundown, they had to walk by us. Because there were only two exits to the room. One leading outside, and the other right by us. And the one by us led to the coach's office and the bins of school-provided sweatpants.

For a while, nothing happened. And then the door opened. "Who's that?" Jenny whispered.

I shrugged. The plan hadn't included anyone else coming in. Especially not Kevin. Who was treading carefully and leading with a stake.

I stifled a yelp and pressed myself back against the wall, my eyes never leaving that sharp piece of wood.

Suddenly, I saw a flash of something, and realized that Chris had just bolted past, a towel wrapped loosely around his hips. He shoved Kevin to the ground as he went, then howled in pain as Kevin sprayed him with holy water from a squirt bottle in his other hand.

Nelson followed, but now Kevin was back up and fully armed—holy water and wood. A lethal combination. He wasn't fast enough, though, and his stake missed Nelson's heart and stuck in his shoulder.

I heard Nelson howl as he raced out into the gym, but I didn't follow. I was a vampire in the boys' locker room with a vampire hunter not ten feet away. Call me crazy, but staying put seemed like the best option.

Unfortunately, it didn't work.

Footsteps. And then Kevin. Right in front of us.

"Beth," he said, ignoring Jenny and Clayton and looking right at me. "Fancy meeting you here."

"Would you believe I walked into the wrong locker room?"

"No," he said. And then he lifted the spray bottle and squirted.

Clayton, bless him, leaped in front of me, but it didn't matter. The spray got me, and it felt like a million fleas had landed on me and were having a picnic.

I bit my lower lip, determined not to scratch. But I think Kevin could tell that I was itching. I mean, why else would his hand go for that stake.

"No!" Clayton yelled, even as I decided that now would be a good time to try a little vampire magic.

"We're not here," I said, looking him straight in the eye and pulling up as much mojo from my gut as I could manage. "You never saw us."

He stared at me, not blinking, his eyes glazed over.

Beside me, Jenny tittered, and out of the corner of my eye, I saw Clayton grab her arm and tug her back toward the wall.

I kept my focus on Kevin. I had to make this work. I might not be a glamour girl, but I intended to pull off this glamour trick if it killed me. (Well, you know what I mean . . .)

"We were *never* here," I repeated.

He swayed a little, his eyes wide, and I started to mentally rack up my victory. Then he smiled, wide and smug, dimples lighting his cheeks. "It's not going to work, Beth."

He lifted the stake, and I braced to run even as Clayton and Jenny cried out "No!" in unison.

And then the stake came down and—
I blinked.
What?

He *sheathed* it. He'd taken the stake and slid it artfully into a camouflaged sheath in his jeans.

"I . . . but . . ." I was stammering, but what else could I do? We'd stupidly trapped ourselves in the corner, and I wasn't going to race out of the room past a man with a stake. Especially since he didn't seem inclined to use it.

"You're not one of them," he said, nodding in the direction Chris and Ennis had fled. "At least not yet."

"How do you—"

"If you were," he said, "the glamour would have worked on me. Not to mention the welts the holy water would have left on your face."

"Oh." He had a point.

He took a step toward me, his hand on the stake. I cringed, my eyes on his hand. "What are you up to, Beth?"

I paused, then decided I didn't have anything to lose. "I'm trying to get my life back," I said.

He seemed to consider that, and then he nodded. "Fair enough." He pulled a business card out of his jacket pocket and held it out to me. "You need anything, you call me."

I took it. I might be shaken, but I was coherent enough to know that a vampire hunter ally might come in handy one day. I started to say thank you, but Kevin wasn't through.

"Just remember that I'm watching you. You turn, and I'll be there." He laid his hand on the stake. "I won't like doing it, but I will end this thing. Got it?"

I nodded. I got it.

I mean, how could I not?

CHAPTER 33

"Okay," Chris said, holding out his hand. "Where is it?"

I was back in the lab, and Clayton was there with me. I took a step backward, and he put his hand on my shoulder. The gesture was totally useless (I mean, the vampiric football god could totally take my geeky sorta-boyfriend), but I still felt better.

"What do you want, Chris?" I asked cautiously. I was expecting him to lay into me about the basketballs. About Nelson getting jabbed in the shoulder. About stealing their clothes (the pictures were already all over the Internet!).

Instead he just squinted at me. "The daywalking formula. You told me to come back for it, remember?"

Duh. With all the excitement after tryouts, I'd totally forgotten. "I told *Stephen* to come back for it," I said. I could hardly put Operation Fry Stephen into place if I couldn't get my "formula" to Stephen!

"And he sent me."

"Nuh-uh," I said. "No way. Steph—"

"Is laying low. I mean, come on! You heard about that vampire hunter, right?"

"So, what? The hunter is keeping Stephen from coming to me?"

"He told me to bring it to him," Chris said. He held out his hand. "Come on. He's waiting."

"*I* told you to send Stephen," I said, holding my ground.

"Damn it, Beth. I already told you! After that fiasco with the vampire hunter, he's keeping a low profile. And he's pissed off, too, you know? Do you really want to be the one to get him more worked up?"

I hesitated. Chris did have a point there.

"Okay," I said. "But this is for Stephen." If Chris got fried, the gig would be up. The school would be short one vampire (which was good), but Bad Boy Stephen would still be around. And that wasn't the way my plan was supposed to go. "So don't get any bright ideas about using it yourself," I added.

"And risk pissing Stephen off? Are you crazy?"

Once again, he had a point.

"Okay, here." I passed him a bottle of Coppertone.

"You're kidding me, right?"

"Um, no."

"This is *sunscreen*."

"Well, sure. It *looks* like sunscreen. But that's the beauty of it. What I've done is enhance the spectrum through the use of the unique properties of our blood. Which means that the particular characteristics of the benzophenones have been enhanced to create a filter that doesn't follow the law of diminishing returns like an ordinary sunscreen." I squared my shoulders and plowed on. "I mean, I can show you the algebraic derivation if you'd like."

He stared at me. For that matter, Clayton was staring at me.

I stared back and waited to see if he'd buy it. The truth was, I was totally bullshitting. But I really had altered the sunscreen. I figured Stephen might take a look at it, so it did have some blood components in there, and a few other odds and ends I'd thrown in for good measure.

None of it was any good, though, if Chris didn't take the bait.

I was beginning to think he was going to call me a big fat liar when he tucked the bottle in his jacket pocket. "Okay, then."

"Just remember—Stephen needs to slather it all over his body. Any bare skin will get fried. And have him wear a hat. His scalp's gonna be a problem."

"Got it."

And then he was gone.

Clayton and I looked at each other, our eyes locked until Clayton finally broke into a wide grin.

"What?" I demanded.

"You," he said. "You are brilliant."

"That's why I'm the valedictorian," I said with a laugh. "And you aren't."

CHAPTER 34

I spent the next twenty-four hours in a state of complete and total freaked-outness, broken only in part by a few nice moments (like Clayton sneaking into my room so that we could watch old *Buffy* episodes on DVD and, you know, make out).

Mostly, though, I was a wreck. Had Stephen tried the stuff? Had he already gone out into the sun and burst into a million bits of dust? Had Janitor Bob swept him up and sent him to the dipsy Dumpster?

I kept hoping . . . but I just didn't know. Partly because nobody was in school who could tell me. Tamara and Stacy weren't around, I couldn't find Chris anywhere, and when I checked after third period on Tuesday, Nelson (though he was surely fully healed by now), was listed as absent in the office attendance records.

Which left me with nothing to do but schoolwork.

A few days ago, that would have been no problem. Now, it felt really weird.

"We'll know soon," Clayton said, sliding up next to me in the journalism room.

"What if he didn't try it?" I whispered. "What if he wants me to demonstrate how to use it?" That little possibility hadn't occurred to me. If I had to slather the stuff on and step outside, *I* was going to be the crispy critter. And I wasn't too crazy about that possibility.

"We'll figure something out," he said. And then he reached out and squeezed my hand. *In public!* With everyone in the room watching.

Oh. My. God.

I *so* have a boyfriend.

Which was exactly what Jenny said to me two periods later as we headed toward Latin. "You freak! Why didn't you tell me!" She whacked me with her notebook and tried to look perturbed. I could tell she was happy for me, though. I mean, lately I'd been having a pretty bad week, what with being a vampire and all. Boyfriend action was a nice little perk.

"Yo! Beth!" A kid I recognized from chess club passed by, his fingers spread in a Vulcan salute. "You and Richie are rocking in the polls."

I turned and blinked at Jenny. "We are?"

"Oh, man! You haven't logged on lately? Tamara and Stacy and Chris and Stephen have *totally* dropped. And you and Richie are climbing fast!" She paused to readjust her books. "I'm not sure you're going to win, though. Richie has totally gone all out. He's started his own blog, and he's posting comments all over the *Watch*."

"About what?"

"About what freaks the popular kids are. About the parties at that bar Stephen took you to. And about how other kids should avoid going because no one can remember what happens there, so maybe they're doing something funny with the drinks. Which isn't true, but it's not like we can tell them the real story, right?"

"Wow," I said, my head spinning. Richie was really making his mark. Which meant that Stephen had to be well and truly pissed.

I made a mental note to buy Richie a present. Like, say, Australia.

I was going to hit Jenny up for more scoop on the blog comments, but the bell had rung, and we were running for our seats. Our Latin teacher, Mr. Tucker, came in—half comatose as usual—and started scrawling vocabulary words on the white board with a dry erase marker.

He stopped when a runner from the office came in and handed him a folded piece of paper. He read it, then looked at me.

"Well, Ms. Frasier. Looks like you're wanted in the gymnasium."

"I am?"

"Take your things," he said, then turned back to the board before I could ask *who* wanted me. Only teachers could pull kids out of class. Ladybell, maybe? Wanting to bust my chops about all my past Stepford articles? Coach Dunne? Because he'd found out I'd gone into the boys' locker room?

On the whole, I didn't want to go. But I was programmed from birth to be a good little student, so I did what all good little students do: I went where they told me to go.

And when I got there, I saw Stephen Wills and Chris Freytag.

Uh-oh.

"Look at this," Stephen said, his face contorted and his voice filled with rage.

I looked.

He was pointing at Chris. Burned, scarred, disfigured Chris. My stomach twisted, and I almost cried out. For that matter, I almost ran. I mean, they had to have brought me there to kill me . . . or worse.

But then Chris gave me just the slightest shake of his head. *Don't say anything stupid,* he seemed to be saying. And he didn't look nearly as pissed off as Stephen. And that didn't make much sense at all.

Since I wasn't at all sure yet what was going on, I decided to say hardly anything at all.

I just looked back at Stephen and waited.

"*This* is what we need you to prevent. *This* is why we made you. And yet we still don't have the formula. We still can't walk during the day!"

"I . . . I . . ." I cleared my throat and tried again. "What happened?"

"I got in a fight," Chris said, his eyes never leaving mine. "And I got shoved outside. They pulled me back in right as my skin was burning, and I yelled something about having gasoline thrown on me. Which was total bs, but it got them out of there."

"When?" I whispered.

"Yesterday. Before dark."

I looked between the two of them. One, Chris had clearly not been in a fight. He'd tried my formula and somehow managed to get out of the sun before he fried. Which begged the question of why my ass wasn't nailed to a wall, but I'd leave that little mystery alone for the moment. My other question was a little more complex. "How come you're still . . . you know . . . scarred?"

"To heal, he must feed. And our food supply has been

rather limited since Richie Carter started his campaign."
Stephen bared his fangs. "But I'll deal with him soon
enough."

"Oh." *Oops.* Give the guy some moxie, and put him in
the line of fire. That *so* hadn't been my plan! "Um, what
about the girls?"

"Drain them so that they can't perform?" He shook his
head. "No. They can use our blood for enhancement. We
cannot use theirs."

I thought that seemed like a goofy rule under the cir-
cumstances, but since Stephen was the big cheese—and
since the big cheese still didn't know that this was all my
fault—I decided to keep my mouth shut.

Except . . .

"My finger healed right away," I said, then told him how
I'd stuck my hand out of the grave.

He brushed off my question. "Your veins flowed with
fresh blood. And your injury was minimal. Even when the
stake burned your hand, the damage was superficial. This,"
he said with a wave toward Chris, "is not."

"It doesn't matter, Stephen," Chris said. "I'll be fine."

"This could happen again," Stephen said, slowly and
calmly. Too calm, if you know what I mean. And I saw the
fury in his eyes when he turned back to me. "Two days.
You have two days to find the answer. Otherwise, my dear,
I think we'll just consider you a lost cause."

CHAPTER 35

"So I guess it's safe to say that your sunscreen formula doesn't work," Chris said. Stephen had left, and we were still in the gym, leaning up against the rock climbing wall.

"I . . . um . . ." Okay, not the best of starts. I lifted my chin and started over. "I did all the research. It should have worked."

"Liar."

Shit. Time to switch gears. "Well, what the hell were you doing putting it on? I told you not to wear the stuff. It was still in an experimental phase."

"Experimental phase my ass," Chris said, taking a step toward me. "You were trying to fry Stephen."

I shook my head vigorously, even as I backed up. "No. No, I wasn't. That would be stupid. And I'm not stupid, right? I mean, I'm the class valedictorian."

"Yeah," he said. "And I used to think that made you totally clueless. But I'm thinking that maybe you're all right after all."

I stopped backing up, my head working hard to keep up with the conversation. "Huh?" And, yes, I know that made me sound more clueless than smart, but, honestly, *huh*?

"I'll help you," he said.

Now he was starting to make me nervous. I felt like one of those bad guys in *Law & Order: Criminal Intent*, certain they were being framed.

I forced a smile, hoping I looked casual about it. "Honest, Chris. I don't know what you're talking about."

"You were hoping Stephen would do exactly what I did," he said. "Slather the stuff on and walk outside. And then he'd go up in a little puff of smoke, and you'd be free."

"So what if I was?" I raised my chin, hoping I sounded more defiant than I felt.

"Well, then, like I said. I'm sorry I messed up your plan." He was wearing cowboy boots—technically forbidden in the gym, but no one much cared at the moment—and now he scuffed his toe across the polished floor. "I had a plan, too. Because that sorry you-know-what pretty much ruined my life."

I gasped, suddenly understanding. He'd truly thought my formula had worked. And he wasn't taking it to Stephen, he was keeping it for himself. If he could daywalk he wouldn't be under Stephen's thumb anymore.

I'd been trying to get revenge. Chris had, too. He just went about it a little bit differently.

"I was supposed to be quarterback," he continued. "And I was supposed to go to college on a scholarship. And I had a girlfriend I liked. And now I'm stuck with that bald bimbo."

I fought back a laugh at his description of Stacy. But I couldn't laugh about what he was saying. "Elise says you were a jerk to her."

"Sure, after Stephen changed me. I mean, I couldn't tell

her. And I sure didn't want her dating a vampire. She's better than that."

"Is that why you're still feeding on her?"

At that, his face flashed with anger. Which was pretty interesting when you consider the fact that he hadn't even gotten angry over the fact that I had (inadvertently, at least) almost killed him.

"What are you talking about?"

"Don't give me that. The marks on her neck. And I know she still likes you. So what are you doing? You're using her by pulling that glamour crap on her and *feeding*! And, man, that is so totally not right!"

I think I was crossing some line here, because even without vampire powers, Chris could pretty much tie me up like a pretzel. But I didn't care. I was pissed. About everything. About me and Elise and the whole damn thing. And it was about time I yelled at someone about it.

Except that yelling at Chris wasn't nearly as satisfying as I thought it would be, mostly because he was staring at me like I'd gone mental.

"I swear I'm not feeding on her. I haven't fed on a person since the beginning."

I frowned at him. "What are you talking about?"

"I didn't know any better," he said. "And Stephen was right there when I clawed my way out of the dirt. With Stacy. And he made me—" He cut himself off and shook his head. "Doesn't matter. But I've been feeding on hospital blood ever since."

"Your dad's a doctor," I said, remembering.

"So's yours."

I nodded. "Yeah. That's all I've had. Bagged blood."

His shoulders slumped. "Guess you're luckier than I am. You still have a chance."

"Yeah," I said. "I hope I do."

"I really do want to help you," he said. "I'll do just about anything to see Stephen taken out."

I thought about what he was saying. There was a chance he was lying—that it was all a trap. But I didn't really believe it. And the truth was, I really did need all the help I could get.

"Okay," I finally said. "Tonight at nine. Meet me at the Home Depot. And bring some cash."

CHAPTER 36

As it turned out, it took more than just one trip to the Home Depot. Clayton and Jenny and Chris and I spent two nights (and Clayton and Jenny spent the days, too) running all over Austin, Round Rock, Pflugerville, Georgetown, Buda, and Kyle hitting every lighting and home improvement store in the area.

My plan was straightforward, but expensive and labor-intensive. We'd had to work our tails off to pull it off before two a.m. on Thursday—the date and time when Stephen had said I better be front and center in the boys' locker room. We'd never officially talked about it, but I guess he knew that I could get into the school after hours. Apparently he could, too. Which wasn't a huge surprise. For that matter, I wouldn't be surprised if he had a lair in the basement or something.

"You should leave now," I said to Clayton once we were all set up. I'd already sent Jenny away. She had one more job to do for us outside, and then she was supposed to go home and stay safe. I think she hated missing the action a little, but I knew that she'd do the job. She had to. Without her, the whole thing could fall apart.

Chris we'd sent away long ago. He'd left to find Stephen and, hopefully, act like all was normal.

"No," Clayton said, in response to my trying to shoo him. "I'm not letting you meet with that guy on your own."

"Ah," a voice said. "Isn't young love wonderful?"

I spun around to find Stephen standing in the doorway, the metal door open to the moonlit football field. I stood stock-still, suddenly afraid he'd want to lead us outside to finish this. But instead he jerked his head, signaling for Tamara and Nelson and Chris to come in around him. Chris, I noticed, entirely avoided looking at me. For a second, I was terrified that it had all been a setup. But then Clayton squeezed my hand and I calmed down. Chris was just afraid Stephen would figure it out. Or, at least, I hoped that was it.

As soon as they were all inside, Stephen let the door shut. I held my breath, knowing that this step was key. Jenny had to be somewhere out there. And unless something had gone terribly wrong, she was slipping the lock through the bolt we'd welded on. Which meant that Stephen and company now had only one way out—through the locker room and into the gym.

I prayed she'd done her job. Because if they disappeared back into the night, my whole plan was shot.

"Do you have it?" Stephen asked. "Or is this where we say good-bye?"

"Of course I have it. You knew I could figure it out."

"I wasn't sure you could manage it so quickly."

"I'm smart," I said. "Ask anyone."

"Believe me. I did." He held out his hand. "The formula."

This time, I'd decided on something a bit more fancy than Coppertone. I'd ransacked my mother's bedroom until I'd found a decorative perfume bottle. And into that I'd poured my concoction. "It's only a start," I said to him as I handed it over. Clayton and I had talked about this, and we'd decided that I'd sound more realistic if I admitted that I hadn't yet totally found the answer. Only an interim solution. "My research suggests there's a permanent cure. But I haven't come up with a workable hypothesis yet."

"And this?" he asked, examining the bottle.

"Completely blocks UV light. That's the culprit, you know. So slather it on, and you're good to go."

"For how long?" he asked, eyes narrowed.

"As far as I can tell, it's good until you shower. But you should probably be careful, at least at first." I figured that was a nice little touch, expressing an appropriate level of concern for my victim.

"I'm impressed," he said.

"Thanks. I—"

"Show me."

I blinked. "What?"

He handed me the bottle, then held out his hand to Nelson, who pulled out a portable black light. And black lights are just oozing with UV rays. Oops.

"Show me," he repeated.

I chanced a look at Chris, who looked as surprised as I felt.

"I . . . well, okay. Sure." My mind was racing, because I really wasn't sure how I was going to manage this one. So I moved slowly. Taking the lid off the bottle. Pouring a tiny bit of my enhanced beach goo into my hand. Rubbing a bit into my hand and forearm.

"It will be morning by the time you finish that," Stephen said.

"I'm just trying to be thorough," I said. "You're not hoping I rush out and get a burn, are you?"

He didn't answer, and I dawdled a bit longer, hoping to buy some time. Didn't work. He held the black light right over my arm and flipped the switch.

My hand burst into flames, and I screamed, jumping back even as Clayton pulled me away. Good thing, too, because suddenly Stephen was right where I'd been, fangs bared, hissing and screaming and swearing that he'd have my heart in his hand.

Behind me, Clayton yanked harder, but I stumbled and fell to the ground, my hand and arm raw beneath me.

That was all Stephen needed, and he leaped on me, his fangs bared. I rolled into a ball, trying to protect my neck, as Clayton kicked and jabbed and tried to keep Stephen away. It wasn't doing any good, though. Nothing was.

Not until I heard Tamara yell, and I looked up to see Kevin burst in from the gymnasium, a crossbow loaded with a wooden stake. He had it aimed right at Stephen's heart, and there was fire in his eyes.

"No!" I screamed, even as he let the thing fly.

I reacted without thinking, grabbing Stephen's belt loop and pulling him down. I couldn't let Kevin kill him. That had to come from me! Anyone else, and I was doomed to stay a vampire.

Kevin looked at me, baffled, but he didn't have time to be confused for long, because Tamara whacked him over the head with the fire extinguisher, and he dropped to the ground, out cold.

"Come on!" Clayton yelled, grabbing my hand and running toward the exit into the gym. I followed, hoping Stephen would take the bait and follow, too.

"Beth!" The warning cry came from Chris, and I turned to find Stephen right there, a stake in his hand.

"You bitch!" he cried, then slammed the stake down. I screamed, expecting the pain . . . expecting to die.

But the stake burst into flames and I was standing there, totally unscathed.

What the . . . ?

"I knew you were a traitor!" That came from Nelson as he leaped toward Chris, and as I turned out of reflex, Stephen launched himself over me and grabbed Clayton.

I reached for Clayton, but it was too late. Stephen had pulled him away. Now he had his fangs bared and on my boyfriend's neck. "Don't even think about moving," he said.

I bit my lower lip nervously, then realized that I'd sprouted fangs of my own—the product, I assumed, of being scared and pissed off.

Beside us, Nelson was still accusing Chris of being a traitor. "I always knew it," he said. "From the moment I saw how hung up you still are on that pansy-ass girl, I could tell. And she doesn't even taste good. What a freakin' waste!"

"*You've* been feeding on Elise?" Chris yelled.

He rushed toward Nelson, leading with a stake. Nelson parried, his own stake out.

Tamara screamed and ran back toward the showers. They collided . . . and as they did, both of their stakes burst into flames. A blanket of fire surged over them, leaving them battered and unconscious on the floor.

I gasped, my hand to my mouth, my eyes half on the spectacle and half on Stephen. I heard Chris moan and knew he was okay. Or he would be. But he was useless at the moment.

I was all alone with a vampire holding my mortal boyfriend hostage. A vampire that I intended to kill because that was the only way to save myself.

Except—

I froze, trembling, as reality smacked me in the head.

"The stake," I whispered. "You tried to stake me and it burst into flames." Wild fury raged through me. "You're *not* my master! You're my equal. So who is? Stephen, *who is my master*?"

I rushed toward him, but he bit down, burying his fangs in Clayton's neck and drinking deep.

Clayton screamed, and my legs went weak. My eyes burned, filling with all the tears I couldn't shed.

"Come closer, and he dies," Stephen said, even with a mouthful of flesh.

"You'll kill him anyway," I whispered.

"Maybe," Stephen said. "But you don't know for sure, do you? And he's my ticket out of here."

He stood then, Clayton limp in his arms, and raced for the back door. I held my breath as he realized it was bolted from the outside. Then he turned, confused, and headed the only direction left to go—out into the gym.

Out into my trap.

I stood perfectly still, hoping it would work. And, more, hoping that if it did, Clayton would be alive to celebrate with me.

And then they were both gone.

I leaped across the room, moving with lightning speed toward the breaker box that controlled the lights in the gymnasium. I had to get there before Stephen got out of the gym.

I reached out—almost there!—and just as I was about to flip the switch, Tamara tackled me from the side.

We rolled across the tile floor, one of her fists pummeling my face and body as the other fumbled for a stake. "You ruined everything!" she cried.

"Me! You're the one who wants to be dead!"

She reached back and came forward, the wood in her hand ominous.

"I don't have time for this!" I shouted. And then—because it just felt so good—I lashed out and punched her in the nose.

She screamed and cupped her nose as blood poured out, the scent of it making my fangs even sharper.

I shoved her off of me and took off running. I could see through the glass in the door that Stephen and Clayton were almost to the far side of the gym, and I launched myself at the light switch, flipped it, then jumped off to the side, afraid that the light filling the gymnasium would get me, too.

At first I couldn't tell if it worked. And then I heard the scream. Low and terrible, it rang out and then silenced abruptly.

I whimpered on the floor, my arms around my knees as I counted to twenty—the number we'd all agreed was the safest.

None of us—not me or Chris or Jenny or Clayton—had been certain how long it would take to burn a vampire. But we figured, with all the UV lights we'd put into the light fixtures at the gymnasium, that it couldn't take too long. Because we'd put enough in that you could get a sunburn in that room.

And surely Stephen couldn't survive that.

The second I hit nineteen, I was on my feet. By twenty, I'd turned the switch off. By twenty-one, I had Clayton in my arms, and by twenty-two, I was back safe in the locker room, just in case Tamara got the bright idea of flipping that switch back on.

But Tamara was long gone. Kevin was still out cold, as were Chris and Nelson.

It was just me and Clayton, and I didn't know what to do.

Because Stephen had drained him.

And if I didn't let him drink from me right then, I knew that my boyfriend was going to die.

CHAPTER 37

I spent the rest of the night and all of the next day huddled in the basement, locked with Clayton's still-as-death body in an unused janitor's closet I'd found.

I'd done it. I'd let him drink. And the moment that it was over, I was certain I'd made a horrible mistake.

I'd condemned him. And I hated myself for it.

Worse, I was afraid he'd hate me, too.

Even worse than that, I knew that it wasn't too late to end it.

And that was why I held a wooden stake in my hand, and part of me knew that I should use it. I couldn't, though.

As horrible as I felt about dumping this whole undead trip on him, I wanted him with me. And I hated myself for being so selfish.

Round and round my thoughts went, ranging from Clayton to a pile of Stephen Wills's ashes in the middle of the basketball court. The lousy little jerkwad had tricked me.

The blood he'd given me in the Bloody Mary hadn't

been his own. But I didn't know whose blood it was—or even if my master vampire was in the school or even in the city.

I'd gotten my revenge, but I hadn't gotten my reward. Worse, I'd made another vampire.

All in all, I wasn't having a really great day.

I needed to fix this. Somehow, I had to find my real master. And somehow, I had to kill him.

Because the only way to make this right was to make Clayton human again. And the only way to do that was to turn myself human.

A chill curled down my spine, and I shivered, realizing that there was one other way. If Clayton killed me—his master—before he drank from a human, then his humanity would be restored.

In front of me, Clayton stirred, and I scurried forward to kneel beside him. "Hey," I said. "It's okay. I'm here. I'm with you."

His eyes were wide, and I knew he was taking it all in. His improved vision. The new awareness in his limbs. "Am I—?"

"I'm sorry."

I waited for him to say that it was okay. That I'd saved him and that he understood and that I'd done the right thing.

He didn't say that, though, and even though I knew it wasn't real, I thought I could feel my heart pick up tempo.

After a second, he reached out and took my hand. And when he smiled, I about melted with relief. After all, he was my boyfriend.

Let me repeat that, just in case you missed it: I, Elizabeth Frasier, had a real, live boyfriend. (Well, an undead boyfriend, anyway.)

I loved him. He loved me.

And vampires don't go around killing the people they love . . . not even to be human again.

Do they?

Beth Frasier has problems. She's undead. Her boyfriend's undead. Her boyfriend could be not undead if he kills her. She's just killed a big-shot vampire, and there's sure to be fallout. And if that weren't trouble enough, she's got final exams coming up. And this whole undead thing is really ruining her college prospects.

Honestly, what's an undead valedictorian to do?

GOOD GHOULS DO

Coming in mass market in August 2009 from Ace Books

NEW IN TRADE PAPERBACK

Saving the suburbs from evil—
one fiend at a time…

Deja Demon

The Days and Nights of a
Demon-Hunting Soccer Mom

**By *USA Today* bestselling author
JULIE KENNER**

Keeping the local kids in line at a neighborhood Easter party will take all of Kate's skills as a mother and Demon Hunter, just when she'll need them the most. An old, very powerful enemy has returned to San Diablo, this time with a full-blown army of the undead and a powerful demonic ally. Once again, it's up to Kate to save the world. Good thing she can multitask…

penguin.com

San Diablo, California.

The perfect place to raise a couple of kids.

And a lot of hell.

Don't miss the first two Demon novels by
JULIE KENNER…

Carpe Demon

California Demon

Praise for Julie Kenner's Demon novels:

"A HOOT!"
—Charlaine Harris

"FABULOUS."
—*The Best Reviews*

"SASSY."
—Richmond.com

M254AS0208

THE ULTIMATE IN FANTASY!

From magical tales of distant worlds to stories of those with abilities beyond the ordinary, Ace and Roc have everything you need to stretch your imagination to its limits.

Marion Zimmer Bradley/Diana L. Paxson

Guy Gavriel Kay

Dennis L. McKiernan

Patricia A. McKillip

Robin McKinley

Sharon Shinn

Katherine Kurtz

Barb and J. C. Hendee

Elizabeth Bear

T. A. Barron

Brian Jacques

Robert Asprin